Also by Mary W. Sullivan

Chili Peppers
Rat Trap
Pancho Villa Rebels
Jokers Wild

THE INDESTRUCTIBLE OLD-TIME STRING BAND

by
Mary W. Sullivan

Publishers since 1798

THOMAS NELSON INC., PUBLISHERS

Nashville   New York

No character in this story is intended to represent any actual person; all the incidents of the story are entirely fictional in nature.

First edition

Library of Congress Cataloging in Publication Data

Sullivan, Mary W.
    The indestructible old-time string band.

    SUMMARY: Five boys who form a string band become unknowingly involved with some criminals who move in next door to the old house in which they practice.
    [1. Mystery and detective stories]   2. Music— Fiction]   I. Title.
PZ7.S9533In   [Fic]   74–34391
ISBN 0–8407–6426–X

48

Contents

The Indestructible Old-Time String Band

The Purple Cow

The first time I paid a lot of attention to Mr. Valentine's place across the street was the day the guys—the Indestructible Old-Time String Band (that's us)—saw his cow. The band was practicing at my house. And my house is in a high-buck neighborhood maybe twelve minutes by freeway from the Los Angeles City Hall.

That Friday, after school, we had sneaked in the back way for a practice session up in my room. We were all there but Bob. He plays mandolin. Late as usual, Bob came in the front way. He's a really good guy—tall, blond—and most times looks as if he were walking in his sleep. Not today. His hair stood up like antennas ready to broadcast. His eyes were wide open. "Errgh!" he croaked.

We all stopped tuning. When Bob has anything to say, we listen. "What's happening?" we asked.

He turned to me. "Frank," he said. "That cow! What's that cow doing there?"

I stared at him. "Cow? Where?"

Bob parted the draperies at my window, peering down to make sure he wasn't dreaming, I guess. Then he stood running his fingers through his hair as the rest of us looked.

I looked. And there on Mr. Valentine's huge lawn, right across the street, tied to a tree near the sidewalk where everyone who passed could see it, was, no fooling, a cow— a dirty old white cow!

Mr. Valentine's house, well . . . ever see pictures of Venice? Not Venice, California—Venice, Italy. They have these palaces on the canals. Mr. Valentine's house is just like that, only instead of on a canal, it's on a little hill. Also, it's a wreck. Windows broken and boarded up and stuff. When I first saw it, I scared myself making up stories about it. I called it the haunted house, sometimes the "haunted palace." But that was a long time ago. I didn't know then what I know now—that it was going to be haunted, and by a mandolin-playing ghost.

Bill, we call him Woody, which is short for his last name, Woodcock, is a little guy with a big voice and dark, furry eyebrows that are all you see at first. He's uptight, really uptight, worries about everything except when he's playing guitar and belting out a song. "Will you look at that!" Woody said. "A cow! And in this high-buck neighborhood!" His eyebrows bunched up.

Tracy just beamed when he saw the cow. He never worries. "What a way to get the lawn mowed!" Tracy's big baby face grinned at us. "And, man, he's sure got some lawn to mow!"

Chester has this wonderful far-out imagination, mostly about music. He kind of looks up into his thick, black-rimmed glasses and gets ideas. He took one look at the cow, picked up his fiddle, began a folk tune and sang:

> I never saw a Purple Cow,
> I never hope to see one;
> But I can tell you, anyhow,
> I'd rather see than be one.

We all cracked up. Purple or not, it was too much. A cow in this neighborhood! But you've got to know about the neighborhood to know how wild, really wild, it seemed.

All the houses here are kind of secret. You could live in one forever and not know who lives next door to you. They're fine, old, well-kept houses with giant trees, high walls, and thick hedges. All you see is gardeners, maids, and expensive cars, often driven by chauffeurs.

Bob was still running his fingers through his hair and looking at the cow chewing away in the long, dry grass. Mr. Valentine's so-called lawn is really a hayfield. Bob said, "That guy would need more than one cow to mow his lawn. He'd need a whole herd."

Chester stared out the window, fingering and bowing his fiddle. He mumbled some words and after a few tries came up with:

> I never saw a Purple Cow,
> Five purple herds, or one;
> But I can tell you, anyhow,
> Some guy is having fun.

"Hey!" I yelled. "How did you know? Maybe you are just making up stuff, but that's got to be it! Mr. Valentine is trying to give us a laugh." I tried to make myself believe it. I'd never seen Mr. Valentine and I was somehow a little scared of him.

Woody's eyebrows came down even farther. "What is he? Some kind of nut?"

I scratched my head, thinking what to tell them. I'd always figured Mr. Valentine had to be some kind of nut to live in a haunted house like that, but I didn't want to let on about being scared of him. "Guess so. That's what Mom says. That's what Mrs. Merrifield, the lady who lives next door to him, says."

Tracy wasn't listening. He moved his bass over next to the window, plucked a low sound, and mooed. We backed him up, mooing at the cow. All of us cracked up when she stopped chewing and looked around.

"Man," Tracy said, laughing. "We've just got to paint her! If she were purple, she'd really be laughs!"

"But," Woody put in. "That nut, that Mr. Valentine . . ."

I was about to agree with Woody when Tracy went on. "Water color put on with brushes won't hurt her," he said, not worrying about Mr. Valentine.

Bob was grinning all over. "The bus goes by here after the game tomorrow!"

That settled it. Tracy took off down the back way to get the paint. We all talked about the laughs the kids would get when they saw a purple cow. Then we started tuning our instruments again and tried the Purple Cow song. After a while we had it down pat and I got them to play "Devil's Dream." I'd been listening to a record, trying to get my picking down perfect on that. It's a great banjo part, and Tracy's bass wasn't too important. The guys backed me up so well I'd almost forgotten about painting the cow when Tracy came back. He handed the can of paint around for us to inspect, but Woody just scowled and wouldn't touch it.

All but Woody looked out the window. The cow was still there, so we left our instruments and started down the front. Mom was in the little phone room with the door open as we sneaked outside. I knew she was talking to Mrs. Merrifield because she was saying, "I hope that cow makes him so conspicuous that the city does something about the mess he's made of that place."

I hadn't thought much about how Mom would feel about our painting the cow, but now I knew it was okay. "Conspicuous," she'd said. Well, if a dirty old white cow was conspicuous, how about a purple cow?

Woody chickened out, of course. He stayed on our side of the street, said he'd be the lookout. And that was good. He signaled when a car was coming, so we could pretend we were just curious kids looking at the cow. And he was keeping a watch on Mr. Valentine to see if he came out of the house.

I guess we were all kind of scared. And the cow! She seemed enormous up close. When Tracy painted her rear, she turned her big, empty-looking eyes at us, stopped chewing and lowered her horns. Maybe she was going to charge! But then she started chewing again and we figured she didn't mind, so we all took a turn with the brush until she was purple, really purple, all over.

We were so interested in getting the cow painted that we forgot about Mr. Valentine. Suddenly there was the bang of a slammed door and we saw Woody's frantic signals to come back. We raced across the street hiding in the bushes that lined the steps to my house. Our hearts were thumping until we saw that Mr. Valentine or whoever had banged the door was gone. Then we began laughing at one another. Just as we were leaving the cow she had flipped her tail and we all had gotten a little purple paint on us. We kind of liked it. How many guys can say they've painted a cow purple? That's the way I felt, anyhow. With the whole band there, I wasn't scared of Mr. Valentine or anybody else. If I had stopped to think, I could have saved us from a lot of trouble.

But then we would have missed all the laughs the next day on the bus. When we got to the block before Mr. Valentine's house, we started the Purple Cow song. Then we pointed out the window. All the kids looked and nearly flipped. They laughed and shoved us around asking questions, but we played it cool. That is, all but Woody. He stuck with us but he didn't like it. "You guys think you're so smart," he said. "Bet this isn't the last we hear of this purple-cow business."

It wasn't.

2

Tracy's Bass

It was in the paper—not about us but about Mr. Valentine, with a picture of his house and purple cow. I read the whole thing. They didn't have a clue. "Mr. Valentine wasn't available for comment," the paper said. The reporters had interviewed the neighbors, who called him an eccentric and a crackpot. It built up my feeling that we lived across the street from a real loony. Of course the paper didn't know we had painted the cow, but because of our song the kids on the bus had gotten the word. We knew that was why they asked us, The Indestructible Old-Time String Band, to play at the assembly a week from Friday.

Man! Did that present problems! First of all, where were we going to practice? After school was okay at my house but to play at assembly needed more practice than that, and just mention "practice" to any of the other guys' parents and they think of all kinds of excuses. To be fair about it, they don't want to disturb their neighbors.

15

The next problem was Tracy and his bass. The trouble was, he didn't have one. The one he used was borrowed; I'd borrowed it for him a long time ago. A bass costs a mint, and Tracy's folks didn't think he needed one.

My banjo was no problem. Gramps knows I like old things, so he left me the old stuff that decorates my room along with this five-string when he and grandmother moved out and started traveling. I took a few lessons from a guy. He taught me to frail, but I didn't learn how to pick until my class went to Disneyland last spring.

The Mad Mountain Ramblers were playing on a wagon in front of the Mine Ride. They play bluegrass—traditional stuff. Ever hear them? Man, once we did—Bob and I—we forgot all about the rides. I'd lucked out getting on the same bus as Bob. Guess I always kind of looked up to him, in more ways than one—he's a lot bigger than I am. Bob and I spent the whole day at Disneyland listening to the Ramblers. Tracy, Woody, and Chester came along one at a time, and got hooked on their music too.

Right after that the five of us decided to have our own string band. But then everyone scattered for the summer, so I spent all vacation keeping myself from being lonesome by learning to pick in the three-finger Scruggs style. Sometimes one or another of the guys would be there, and just before school started we got it all together. Then Tracy had to have a bass.

I remembered Mrs. Flanigan had a bass behind the grand piano in her living room. Mrs. Flanigan has this enormous house. a couple of blocks away, and about a dozen kids. I asked Curtis, the one who used to be my friend, if we could borrow his mom's bass, and he said,

3

Mr. Valentine

We raced down, across the street, past the purple cow, the No Trespassing signs, and up the hill. We picked our way through the heaped-up lumber and boxes by the front door, and there was Mr. Valentine waiting for us. He didn't look weird at all. After filling his pipe he tucked the pouch into the pocket of his tweed sports jacket and, smiling and bowing slightly, pointed to the open front door with his pipe. He was tall and athletic looking and no slob.

Inside we all stopped to gawk. We were in a great cool hallway with a floor of black-and-white marble tiles, like a giant checkerboard. Rows of tall, dark chairs of wood stood against walls hung with huge gold-framed mirrors. The room on one side was dim and crammed with what looked like covered-up furniture. On the other side of the hall the room was filled with packing boxes. There, leaning against one of the packing boxes, with the light shining on it, was a beautiful old beat-up bass.

We stopped by the bass and Mr. Valentine introduced

21

himself. "I'm James Valentine," he said in a deep voice as politely as if he were talking to my dad.

I stepped forward. "I'm Frank Corbett," I said. "I live across the street."

He smiled, bowing slightly. "How do you do, Frank." Maybe he didn't try to shake hands because of my banjo. He just looked at it and grinned, "Frank Corbett, banjo."

I turned to Bob next to me. "Mr. Valentine, this is Bob Norton."

He bowed and smiled at Bob. "And Bob Norton, mandolin."

He went on like that to Chester and Woody. When he came to Tracy, he said, ". . . and Tracy Fields, bass, I presume. You caught me just in time, Tracy." He nodded toward the packing boxes. "I'm moving up the hill." He waved his pipe vaguely in the direction of the mountains. "Now bring the bass and I'll listen to you in here."

I can't forget the look on Tracy's face when he laid his hands on that bass. He looked like a little kid who'd found just what he'd dreamed of under the Christmas tree. His hair is fine and silky, and I noticed the shine of his hair against the blond wood of the bass as he rubbed his hand up and down its neck.

Then I saw how Mr. Valentine watched him with an amused smile. I had liked him up to then, such a gentleman and all but, well, suddenly he looked sort of sly.

He led us down the hall and Woody, just ahead, turned to me with his eyebrows down. "You call the shots," he whispered. Woody usually tells us what tunes to play, so he was passing the buck to me. I thought about it as we followed along outside across a patio full of dried-up leaves, tin cans, and broken bottles. Mr. Valentine unlocked a

door in the other wing, on Mrs. Merrifield's side of the
house, and we were in a large dim room with the windows
half broken and half boarded up. There was nothing in
there but a long, heavy wood table with carved legs,
which was covered with dust and some yellowed newspapers.

Mr. Valentine used a piece of the newspaper to dust off
a corner of the table to perch on. He cupped his pipe in his
hand, lighted up, then waved the stem at us and said,
"Now, let's hear you play."

We tuned up. Everyone's eyes bugged at the deep, rich
sound as Tracy brought the bass to life. Then we were
ready and I said, "We'll play 'Daybreak in Dixie.'" That's
a light, tricky instrumental—lots of mandolin. Seemed to
me to be the kind of thing Mr. Valentine would appreciate.
But I couldn't tell if he liked it or not.

Next we played "Devil's Dream." That's another instrumental.

"Very good," he said, but I wasn't sure he meant it.
"Know any songs?"

"How about 'Uncle Pen'?" I said. We lit into that and he
seemed to like it better. I decided to pull out all the stops
on the next one. We sang "Black-Eyed Susy," a song with
some funny words that gives Woody a chance to really belt
it out. I watched Mr. Valentine when Woody sang:

> Wish I had a sweetheart
> I'd put her on the shelf
> And every time she smiled at me
> I'd get up there myself.

Mr. Valentine didn't smile, but just when we finished I

heard a sound like a window closing near by. Then I saw
that Mr. Valentine seemed to be studying us instead of
listening.

Suddenly he stood up, said, "Very good, boys. Very
good," and started for the door. We followed.

Then Tracy said, "What shall I do with the bass?"

Mr. Valentine turned around. "Leave it here. Take it
with you. It's yours—I don't care."

Almost overcome with joy, Tracy thanked him.

Mr. Valentine took another step toward the door. "Leave
it here if you boys want to come back and practice."

We all looked at each other in amazement, not daring
to believe what we had heard.

Chester, being logical, nailed him. "You mean you'll let
us use this room for practice?" His voice came out all high
and incredulous.

"Certainly," said Mr. Valentine sort of impatiently.
"Anytime—anytime at all. I won't be here." He stopped
to flip the light switch. Nothing happened. "Better bring
along a light bulb if you come at night."

"At night?" we gasped.

"Certainly," he said. "You're perfectly welcome." I
could only see his back, but I thought he was looking sly
again.

We thanked him and thanked him. Then we practically
had to unglue Tracy's hands from that bass. It seemed to
the rest of us that by leaving it we staked a claim to the
room. And it would look as if we didn't trust Mr. Valentine
if we took it.

He was waiting for us out on the patio. When we joined
him, he locked the door and tossed the key to me. "You
may come and go this way." He pointed with his pipe to

a faint path through the dead weeds and grass that led to the side street. "Just you five. No other boys, you understand." His manner made it clear that it was time for us to go. "It's been a pleasure meeting you boys," he said with his formal little bow. "I'll be around from time to time."

"It's been a pleasure meeting you, too, Mr. Valentine," we said. "And thank you again."

Tracy stopped by him as the rest of us started down the path. "Mr. Valentine," he said. "I can never thank you enough." Anyone could tell it came from the very bottom of Tracy's heart.

At the very last there, Mr. Valentine's patience seemed to give out. He had no time for Tracy, he just pointed with his pipe.

I really wondered if he meant it about the room.

4

Our Own Room

We didn't waste any time after school the next day, and sure enough, the key unlocked the door. It was great having our own room for practice. All of us guys agreed not to tell the other kids. Our families were pretty stunned about it, but as Mom said, ". . . after all, it's right across the street."

It didn't seem like right across the street. It seemed like another, unreal kind of world. When we looked our room over, we saw that the plaster was all water-stained around the windows and hanging down from the ceiling in big hunks. The door leading into the main house had a board nailed across it and we could see that the knob had been taken off. I felt somewhat better about that. Mr. Valentine had said he would be around from time to time, and this way he couldn't just walk in on us. In one corner of the room, by a stack of lumber, we found a mess with feathers where some poor little bird had flown in and died. The

27

room was dim and shadowy, with the windows partly boarded up and all. Kind of spooky, really.

We didn't see Mr. Valentine that first week, but the cow was still there. No one had ever walked along the sidewalk much before, but now someone was always looking at the cow when we went in. Children's nurses in uniforms stopped with little kids; a guy was there with a camera; boys and girls on bikes rode by and mooed at the cow.

Then, on Thursday, Tracy, Chester, and I were coming down my front steps. Chester had left his fiddle at my house, and I had to get my banjo. Bob and Woody were waiting with their instruments and watching the cow. Two young gangster-type characters came walking along gawking up at Mrs. Merrifield's. When they got to Mr. Valentine's and saw the cow they did a double take.

They started laughing and quizzing Bob. We could see him come awake answering their questions. Then the hoods laughed again and Woody slugged Bob in the arm. Bob looked down at Woody, ran his fingers through his hair, but kept on talking.

By the time we got over there the two hoods were turning the corner and Woody was giving Bob the business. His eyebrows were down a mile. "You big lug! Can't you keep your mouth shut!"

"Shh. Look!" Tracy whispered.

Just around the corner a black Cadillac had pulled up. A door opened and a man's harsh voice called, "Find out anything?"

"Sure," the hoods answered. They hopped in and the car sped off.

"See! What did I tell you?" Woody said to Bob.

We started up the path. "What's the beef about?" we asked.

Woody was telling us the questions the hoods had asked about the cow, the house, and who lived there. Bob stopped him. "Errgh," he croaked. "The rest was okay, but I shoudn't have told them Mr. Valentine moved out."

"You told them that?" I said. I didn't mind the laughs about the cow, but, well, now that I'd met Mr. Valentine, I knew that, sly as he was, he wouldn't have wrecked his house. He might not be able to keep up the yard, but the inside—that beautiful hall. I couldn't see him breaking his own windows. And the cow? The cow wasn't there for laughs. If Mr. Valentine had a sense of humor, it wasn't showing the day we met him. Maybe he had the cow out front to make it look as though someone lived there. And Bob had spilled the beans to those hoods.

Chester was being logical. "Forget it," he said. "You told them. So forget it and hurry up." He looked up into his glasses. "I've got a fiddle tune you guys won't believe. It'll go over big with the teachers. It's 'Richmond Cotillion.' "

The next night was Friday. Our folks said we could stay in our room until ten o'clock that night, so we got the biggest light bulb we could find and started over. It was dark when we went up the path, and perfectly quiet. All the guys must have felt the heavy silence because they began to whisper, as if someone who might hear us were inside the house. I may have started the running, lightly, on tiptoe, to get to the safety of our room. With the key in my hand I reached the door first. The other guys, rustling the dry leaves and stumbling over bottles and cans, came up behind me. I stood there shaking, looking into the threatening blackness of our room. The door was wide open!

I knew I had locked it. After all the trouble getting Tracy's bass, I wasn't about to take any chances with it. Tracy pushed by me and disappeared into the blackness. Bob lighted a match and held it over my shoulder so we could find the cord with the old bulb hanging from it.

Then the match went out. We heard that high tremolo violin note that goes on and off in horror movies. Chester and his whacky imagination! Maybe because we were scaring ourselves then we didn't know the difference when we should have been scared.

But Chester's joke broke the ice. Tracy yelled, "It's here! It's okay!"

I found the cord, screwed the old bulb out and the new one in, but it's a wonder I didn't get electrocuted, my hands were so sweaty. When the light came on, we all stood around laughing with relief.

Woody stopped laughing first and pulled his eyebrows down at me. "What's the idea—not locking the door? Scared the hell out of me! Anything could have been hiding in that dark room!"

"But I did lock it!" I told him. "Scared the hell out of me too."

"And me," Bob said.

"Then who left it open?" Woody asked. "Mr. Valentine kept it locked. He wouldn't have."

"He could have," Chester said. "It's his house. He can do what he wants around here." Chester was mumbling. He'd tucked his fiddle under his chin and started tuning.

No one had a better answer, so we let it go at that. We

worked on "Richmond Cotillion." When we got that down pretty well we stopped for a rest and to eat some cookies Bob's mom had sent. It was kind of quiet with just our chewing and we began to hear a scratching sound. It was coming from the other end of the room—either from the boarded-up window or from the door to the main house.

Woody looked panicked. "What's that?" he whispered.

"Aw, just a rat," Tracy told him. "We get rats out at my uncle's stable all the time. They sound just like that."

The scratching noise became a clawing noise. It was something much bigger than a rat. It was coming up the outside of the boarded-up window.

"That's no rat!" Woody said, huddling up to his guitar, his big dark eyes glued to the place where the sound came from. We all sat there terrified. Then slowly over the top of the boards came first one ear, than the nose of Mac, our big striped tomcat. I'd forgotten to give him his dinner and he had come to get me.

Mac plopped down into the room and everyone folded with laughing. Bob tried to feed him a cookie, but Mac won't eat cookies. Then we put him in the middle of the table and, watching us, he curled up to wait for me to go home and feed him. It was about nine fifteen then.

Woody was still nervous and asked for the key to the door. He tried to laugh and pretended to shake as he locked us in. "I'd feel a lot safer if I knew nothing bigger than a tomcat could get in!"

Then we started on the songs. We were in the middle of "New Camptown Races" when there was a banging at the door.

A high-pitched man's voice shouted, "What's going on in there?"

We had listened carefully to everything Mr. Valentine had said and it didn't sound at all like him.

We looked at Bob.

"Errgh! Who—who are you?" he shouted in his bass voice.

The door handle rattled and Woody was looking pleased with himself when we heard a key being fitted into the lock and the door flew open.

There stood a policeman with his revolver leveled at us!

5

Officer Bryant

The policeman's quick blue eyes darted around at us from under his white helmet until he seemed to have the picture. Then he put his gun away and strode in, looking a little weighted down with his heavy dark clothes, boots, gun and all, but sharp and efficient. He was a short, wiry guy about as old as Tracy's big brother. "What's going on here?" he demanded. "Don't you kids know you are trespassing?"

Tracy always has the nerve. "How can we be trespassing when Mr. Valentine gave us the key?" he asked.

The officer threw him a withering look. "Now I reckon you know as well as I do that Mr. Valentine wouldn't give out a key to any kids. Let's see your key."

I got the key from Woody and handed it to him. "You can ask my dad. He's right across the street," I said.

I guess I shouldn't have said it.

The policeman stuffed the key into his pocket and

spoke angrily. "Across the street! Just about what I thought! Kids around here have no respect for other folks' property. Vandals!" He waved his hand at the broken windows. "Look at what they did while he was away! Mr. Valentine told me about it. I gave him my word I'd watch his house for him. The lady next door called saying boys were making a racket over here. And here you are! I caught you in the act!"

This was too much for Chester's logical mind. He stared through his thick glasses at the police officer. "Caught us in what act?" His voice was high and shrill. "Caught us in the act of playing 'New Camptown Races.' So how does that hurt Mr. Valentine's house?"

The officer glanced around at our instruments. Then he pushed back his helmet a bit and scratched behind his ear. He didn't answer Chester. "Where's Mr. Valentine?" he asked.

At first I thought no one was going to answer him and I didn't dare after throwing him into such a fit. We all looked up at Bob.

"Errgh. He moved—er, up the—er, hill."

"That's what he said." Tracy mimicked Mr. Valentine's low voice and gesture with his pipe. "I'm moving up the hill."

The officer looked down and pursed his lips the way teachers do when they don't want to smile. Then he sprang into action. He grabbed Bob, the biggest, by the arm. "I'm right sorry, boys, but I've got to run you out of here until I get in touch with Mr. Valentine. Now! Get a move on!"

"Okay, okay!" we said. We started putting our instruments in their cases. Mac dropped down off the table to follow me but getting home took us a while because we had to wait for Tracy, who was lugging his bass. We took it along because we didn't know if we would ever get back into our room again.

But the next morning Mom called me and I was glad I had told her about getting run out by the policeman. There he was standing at our front door.

He grinned at me. "I'm right sorry about what happened last night. Reckon I owe you an apology." He dug into his pocket and handed me back our key. "That Valentine guy has me stumped. First he hates all kids, then he turns over his house key to a string band!" He shook his head.

"Yeah," I had to agree. "He's pretty hard to figure." I felt kind of strange talking to him like this after last night. Still he seemed to want to be friendly, so I told him about Mr. Valentine's giving Tracy the bass.

"I saw it," he said. "It's a beauty. When Mrs. Merry-what's-her-name, next door, called about you boys I went in there."

I heaved a big sigh of relief. "Then you must have left the door open!"

He grinned. "Reckon you're right. I figured you were coming in those broken windows and tried to trap you by leaving the door open. I was pretty surprised to find the door locked later on." He turned to look across the street at Mr. Valentine's house. "Mr. Valentine said my call put him in mind of some work he has to do down here. Sure could use some!" He shook his head.

We both looked. Mrs. Merrifield's yard was almost hidden in greenery. Even her driveway, all that separated her house from Mr. Valentine's, disappeared into a tunnel of trees. By contrast Mr. Valentine's yard, besides the dry grass and cow, had only shrubbery gone wild and dead trees reaching up gray claws. It looked awful.

"Say, your name is Frank, right? I'm Officer Bryant. I should have known after seeing the bass that you had a band in there, but all I could think of when I came up last night was a stereo. You kids sounded good—real good."

I felt as if Officer Bryant had handed me a plateful of hundred-dollar bills. I looked at him in disbelief. He really meant it! I guess I showed in my face that I was pleased. Before I could say anything he went on. "Can you kids play 'Orange Blossom Special'?"

"We're working on it," I said.

"I go for that country music," he said. "I really do."

I didn't want to be rude, so all I said was, "Yeah."

"Never miss the Gran Ole Opry," he said. "Ever been to Nashville? Country music's made that town. Folks say it's a multi-million-dollar business."

"I've heard of it," I said. "I only listen to Gran Ole Opry when Flatt and Scruggs or Bill Monroe are on." I didn't like to tell him what I thought of all that hokey sequin stuff and electrified instruments. "You see," I said, "we don't plug in. We play bluegrass. Do you know about that?"

He kind of shook his head. "But I know about not plugging in. We did a right lot of front-porch, back-porch singing and picking in the part of Carolina I come from."

"You did!" I couldn't help showing how excited I was. "That's what I mean!" I said. "Old-time music, traditional stuff."

"That's what you call bluegrass? You bet your sweet life I know about that stuff!" Suddenly he looked worried and checked his watch. "I've got to go," he said. He started down the front steps, calling back to me: "You kids going to be there tonight? I'm off duty. I'll teach you boys some of that old-time, traditional stuff you're talking about."

"We'll be there!" I yelled after him, forgetting he was a cop.

Swain County Music

I really shook the guys up when I called them. All of them could come but Tracy. He was going across town to the Ashgrove with his brother to hear Doc Watson.

I tried to talk him out of it. "Maybe this guy is another Doc Watson," I said. "And you'd get to play bass for him."

"I'll take my chances," Tracy said.

Officer Bryant had his guitar with him when he came. Dressed like the rest of us in T-shirt, jeans, and sneakers, he could have been one of the group.

First we tried out "Orange Blossom Special" for him. Chester does a terrific job of fiddling on this, and all in all we get to feeling like it's a real steam train wheel-clacking around the bend. Officer Bryant joined in and we all knocked ourselves out keeping up that driving locomotive rhythm.

After that we relaxed awhile and Officer Bryant started

playing his guitar. "You know this one?" He started singing in that tense, high, vibrant way we try so hard to imitate.

The guys went wild over his singing, and between songs Officer Bryant told us about how it was back in Swain County, North Carolina. He told us about Uncle Dan, who was older than God, tottering down from his mountain to play in fiddle contests—and win. He said Uncle Dan knew more hoedowns, reels, jigs, and hornpipes than anyone had ever heard of. He remembered them from his old kinfolk, who brought them over from the British Isles.

He told us about barn dances, even church music, and how it was singing and picking on porches and in front of log fires. He sang songs that resembled old newspapers, telling about things that had happened and about people; like the one about the lost woman flyer, Amelia Earhart, that Woody insisted on trying to learn.

We felt as if we were there with him in Swain County instead of in our room with one light bulb, windows broken and boarded up, and the ceiling falling down. I had to tell him. "I wish I could live where people are like that—so kind of sincere and natural and friendly."

Officer Bryant laid his guitar on the table and stared at me. "Well, I don't reckon it's so much different from right here." He looked around at the guys.

I looked too. Bob was wide awake listening and running his fingers through his hair. Behind Chester's glasses his face expressed understanding of what I had said. Woody's eyebrows were up for once, and his big eyes were full of fun.

Officer Bryant grinned. "I don't know that those peo-

ple back there are any more sincere and natural and
friendly than this group right here."

Chester tried to help me out. "Frank doesn't mean that
we aren't okay. It's just that the music—"

"Yeah," Woody said. "We all like the same kind of music
but other people don't." He looked up at Bob.

"When we play we get into each other's heads," Bob
said.

Officer Bryant grinned. "I get it." He scratched behind
his ear. "And back in Swain County, where it was the
only kind of music we had, maybe we did get into more
heads and feel closer." He sighed. "Sure do miss it."

I didn't say anything, but I felt good to hear the guys
saying all that. It came to me that we didn't have to be in
Swain County to feel a kind of front-porch, back-porch,
log-fire closeness. It existed right here in our own room.

On the way out we told Officer Bryant we had been
asked to play at assembly. We thanked him for coming,
and the next day when we got together for practice all we'd
learned from him really came out.

I can't explain what happens on a day like that, but we
all seemed to be, as Bob had said, in each other's heads,
and our playing blended together to make sounds so wonderful and wacky and exciting that we were bug-eyed with
joy. We couldn't believe our own ears.

As we were leaving we decided to get something old-
fashioned to wear—sort of a trademark for the Indestructible Old-Time String Band to try out at assembly. Also
we'd get a new set of strings to put on our instruments
a couple of days before we played. Chester told us that
would give the strings time to stretch and adjust. What if

we were all up there on the stage playing and a string snapped! Then we worked out a balanced program, leaving "Richmond Cotillion" for last, so the teachers wouldn't think we were too zany.

Monday, after school, when we were walking down the sidewalk in front of my house, we had the idea about the glasses. We would get some old-fashioned gold-rimmed spectacles at the Salvation Army Store or someplace; we wouldn't have time really to dress up before the assembly.

All of a sudden Bob said, "Look!" He was staring at Mr. Valentine's front yard.

"Where's the cow? What's he building there?" Chester asked. He's nearsighted even with his glasses.

"It looks like those packing boxes he had for moving," said Tracy.

"Yeah," I agreed. "That's what those are. But how did his station wagon get down there?"

Right in the middle of the whole mess of packing boxes, on a sort of ledge, was the old beat-up station wagon. It had long ago lost most of its paint. Just a few patches of bright blue hadn't peeled off, but most of the wood paneling had. The windows all were either cracked or broken, and the way it tilted some of the tires were flat.

"Let's go see what's coming off!" yelled Tracy, starting across the street.

"Tracy! Hold it!" Woody warned.

We had never gone off the path Mr. Valentine had pointed out to us, so we all held back.

"If we go up there, the neighbors might think we did it," Woody explained. "Maybe that's the plot. To blame us for the wreck the place is in."

"There was enough stuff wrecked already if he wanted to blame it on us," Chester reminded him.

Then I remembered something. "Mr. Valentine told Officer Bryant he had some work to do down here. Maybe he's around in back."

We took off to the side street and up our path, looking the place over. The cow was gone and Mr. Valentine wasn't there.

"Wait!" Bob stopped us before we went into our room. "Maybe that junk was the work he had to do!"

We all looked at each other because, of course, that must be it! We didn't have such a good practice that day. We just couldn't figure what was going on.

7

Assembly

By the next day we began to think all that stuff Mr. Valentine had dumped on the front lawn was funny. The tension let down.

"So what? I just hope he doesn't make a project out of working on our room," I said.

"Or on my bass," Tracy said, rubbing his cheek against it and fooling around with the tuning.

Then Bob pulled a package out of his mandolin case. "Look what I found for us."

He had five pairs of old gold-rimmed spectacles. We all put them on and laughed at each other. Funny how a little thing like that can change your whole look. Chester had to take off his own, but he doesn't need to see to play the fiddle.

Then Tracy had an idea. "We'll go out on stage at assembly without the glasses. All at the same time you put on yours. I'll pat all my pockets looking for mine, then make a big thing out of reaching down and unhooking

45

them from the bridge of my bass." He showed us how he could do it. We thought it was pretty funny. Just the kind of gag we needed to break the ice at assembly.

We were getting so keyed up about our act that we forgot all about Mr. Valentine for the next few days.

By the time assembly came on Friday, we were all nervous wrecks. My handkerchief was permanently wet from wiping off the sweat that appeared on my hands every time I thought about it.

We had to sit in the front row with our instruments, waiting for the principal, Mrs. Dobbs, to make the announcements and then for the pep commissioner to tell us about the next game. It seemed endless. We had already tuned our instruments, and any little change in temperature can put them out of tune. But just when I was beginning to get frantic, thinking we should be backstage or someplace tuning, Mrs. Dobbs came out again and said, "Now some of our students are going to play for us." She looked down at her notes. "I present the Indestructible Old-Time String Band."

The kids clapped.

I figured to start tuning on the way up the steps, so I began on my banjo as I led the way. I could hear the rest of the guys doing the same behind me. Then I heard a kind of thump, the kids in the audience giggled, and I knew Tracy had managed to trip with his bass.

On stage we finished tuning, each of us looking at Chester when we thought we were okay. Chester has perfect pitch. Then we put on our spectacles and Tracy went into his act. The kids cracked up just the way we'd hoped they would. We were starting to feel more relaxed.

Woody, sounding really casual, announced, "We'll start off with 'Black-Eyed Susy.' "

It's a frailing number for me on the banjo, much easier than a lot of fancy picking. We got some applause and began to feel warmed up.

Woody tossed in a remark before announcing the next number. He said, "Get off the stove, Grandma. You're too old to ride the range."

The kids loved that. Then we played "Cornbread, Molasses, and Sassafras Tea." Bob stepped forward for the mandolin part and they broke in with some applause; then I did my fast banjo picking part and they clapped again. We played a funny song: "Beware, Oh, Take Care," and finished off with "Richmond Cotillion," the one for the teachers. Right then the bell rang. The kids clapped on the way out, some of them gathering around as we put our instruments away to tell us how good we were.

We had to hurry to get to class. I couldn't believe it. All day long kids and even teachers kept telling me how well we'd played.

Woody had to go to the dentist, but the rest of us couldn't wait to get back to our room after school. We had assembly to talk over and the kids had told us about a contest at the Poverty Palace, a coffeehouse uptown. They thought we should try out for it.

When we got to Mr. Valentine's we saw a moving van next door having problems coming down the driveway with Mrs. Merrifield's stuff. Mr. Valentine was standing on the sidewalk and Officer Bryant on his cycle was pulling up at the curb. He beckoned to us and we stood around waiting as he talked to Mr. Valentine.

Mr. Valentine had been watching the van when we first saw him. He looked as sharp as ever but instead of a pipe in his hand, he had a string of padlocks hooked over his finger. He didn't even seem to know us but we were all very polite and said, "Hello, Mr. Valentine." I'd thought Mr. Valentine would be pleased to see Mrs. Merrifield moving out. They hadn't seemed very friendly. Now, I saw that he was too worried to notice us. "I'm locking up," he told Officer Bryant. "Saw some of those hooligans around here again." He looked back up at his house. "I've still got some valuable stuff in there. Couldn't take it all with me."

Officer Bryant took out his notebook. "The kids here tell me you've moved. Want to give me your new address?"

Mr. Valentine got that sly look. "Just as well keep that a secret," he said. "They're out to get me, you know." He moved over to look at Officer Bryant's notebook. "You've got the number of my answering service. That will do just as well."

"Don't worry," Officer Bryant told him. "I'll keep an eye on the place. And the boys, here . . ." He turned to us. "You kids will tell me if you see anything out of line?"

"Sure," we said.

But Mr. Valentine didn't look happy at all. In fact he didn't even look friendly. He just turned around and hurried back up to the house with the padlocks jangling on his finger.

Officer Bryant watched him go. He tipped his helmet back a bit and scratched behind his ear. "There's a man with a persecution complex or something. Have you seen anyone around here?"

Tracy spoke up. "Not since he took his cow away."

Bob said, "Errgh," but I was so anxious to tell Officer Bryant about the assembly and the Poverty Palace, I butted in. If Woody had been there he would have told him about those two gangster-type guys and the black Cadillac. Me and my big mouth! But ever since the night when officer Bryant played with us, I'd felt our room was a kind of warm, happy place where we would always be safe. I told him about assembly.

Officer Bryant slapped his leg and laughed. "You're telling me those kids really went for that country stuff?"

I corrected him. "Bluegrass."

He nodded and shrugged. "Reckon you're right, but I bet those kids don't know the difference."

I told him about the Poverty Palace. He knew where it was, said to let him know when we'd be playing there. Then he glanced at his watch and jumped on his motorcycle. "I'll check you out up there, too," he said, nodding up at Mr. Valentine's and stomping down to start his bike.

We all turned around and raced up the path to our room. When we got to where we could see Mr. Valentine's front door, we saw him laying something on the front seat of a new blue Porsche.

Slowing down to keep it quiet, we walked lightly toward our room. We'd gotten the message that he wasn't too happy about our being there.

We were probably all thinking about the gleaming blue Porsche—some change from the old station wagon. I know I was thinking about it when we got in sight of our door. We all took a double take. What a jolt! There was a shiny new hasp, ready for a padlock, on our door.

"Whispering"

After practice we looked at the hasp again. Then we looked to see if Mr. Valentine's blue Porsche was there. It wasn't.

Tracy was jubilant. "Anyway my bass is at school; he can't take that back." He'd had to leave it there after assembly until his brother could pick it up. "If Mr. Valentine puts the padlock on, I've still got my bass!"

I was glad of that, of course. But our room! It meant a lot to me. Even with all the glow from assembly, I had a low feeling. I forgot it for a while at dinner when Mom asked me about assembly.

She and Dad seemed to think it was great that the kids liked us so much. They asked questions about it and about the Poverty Palace. I wanted Mom to know about the Poverty Palace because she would probably be the one to drive us. Then I began to get the feeling Mom and Dad weren't all that interested. I changed the subject and asked Mom about Mrs. Merrifield, and where she and all her aunts had gone.

Then Mom really came to life. "Can you believe it?" she asked Dad. "Elsa Merrifield sold that house. Right off, without any problem at all. And I've been thinking houses that big would be impossible to sell."

Dad looked at her. "They are, you know. Why, I've seen them sit for years with 'For Sale' signs in front of them. She was lucky, very lucky. Either that or she gave it away."

I could see Dad was pretty interested, too, so I asked, "Who bought it?"

"Let's see," Mom said. "Seems to me she said the name was Rose."

"Big family?" Dad asked.

"Elsa doesn't know anything about them. The real-estate people handled the whole thing." Mom looked at me. "With your friend, Mr. Valentine, next door, it's a miracle the house was sold at all."

Dad and Mom went on talking about how eccentric Mr. Valentine was and what a wreck his place was and all, and what it did to real-estate values.

I began worrying about him, too, and about the hasp he'd put on our door. I knew I couldn't sleep until I knew if a padlock was on. My pen was there. I'd left it when I wrote down the words to "Rovin' Gambler." I had another pen, but it was a good excuse. I told my folks about it and asked if I could go get it. They said okay.

But just as I was going out the door, the phone rang. I charged back to answer it. It was Woody with some ideas about what to play at the Poverty Palace. When I came out of the room where the phone is I heard Mom and Dad talking about me. They thought I had gone.

Dad was saying, ". . . I don't care what you say. Boys his age should be getting interested in cars. I did. What's he going to do? Spend his whole life strumming that banjo?"

"Not 'strum,' " Mom said. " 'Pick,' or 'frail.' Rita Flanigan tried to explain. Her boy, the one just younger than Curtis, Frank's friend, started the same kind of band." Mom sighed. "I must say she's learned a lot more about it than I have. I'm giving too much time to my guild work."

"What difference does it make?" Dad said. "The sooner he gets off this music kick, the better, as far as I'm concerned."

Mom just laughed. "Oh, music's good for the soul. But I do wish they'd play something I've heard before. All this old-time stuff! Now take the old music we heard as we grew up. Like 'Whispering.' "

Dad laughed and tried to sing it in his shaky bass. "I forget the words," he said. "A good song."

"Mmm, really good," Mom said. "I can still hear those high violins when we danced to it at the Huntington." Her voice was getting all corny and high and girlish. "Makes shivers go up and down my spine."

I'd eavesdropped about enough. My mom and dad are both big and dignified. I get embarrassed for them when they talk like that. I slipped out the back. But I made a mental note of that song. Maybe Chester knew it. If we could learn "Whispering," maybe Dad wouldn't think we were so wacky.

I was worrying about Dad and Mom as I jogged along over to Mr. Valentine's. All at once I noticed how dark it was. I had never been over there alone at night. It was the kind of darkness with a far-off moon making everything look all different grays, and just black in the shadows. When I got to the top of the hill and saw Mrs. Merrifield's house all dark, too, I really tensed up, scuffing hard at the leaves, bottles, and cans in the patio to let myself know it was okay to be there.

First of all, I looked at the hasp on our door, and it was just the way it had been when we left. No padlock. What a relief! Then I forced myself to go into the shadows to see the other door that opened onto the patio, and, sure enough, it was padlocked.

I felt safe again when I got into our room with the light on. The pen had slipped into the newspapers, and it took me a while to find it. When I did, I realized I'd been there quite a long time. I dashed out, locking the door without looking around. When I turned, my way was blocked. My eyes came to about belt-buckle high on a huge man!

As I looked up, his black trousers seemed to come almost to his armpits. The white sleeves of his shirt caught the moonlight. When my eyes reached his long, hard face, I saw that he was staring at me as if I were something that had crawled out of the woodwork. I felt about two inches high.

"Where'd you get that key?" he growled. "You live here or something?"

I shook my head and stuffed the key in my pocket.

"What are you doing here?" he asked, reaching toward me. His hand looked like a big clamp.

I tried to dodge around him but he grabbed me, clamping his hand on my arm. It hurt and I tried to scream, but the sound hardly came out at all, I was so scared.

The man grinned a dirty grin down at me and shook me

until I was dizzy. "Scram! Scram!" he shouted into my face, blasting my eardrums. "And don't let me ever catch you around here again!"

He threw me down on the ground and stood back with that evil grin. He took a puff on his cigar that lit up his face, sort of pinkish—like Frankenstein. Then he plucked the cigar out of his mouth with his thumb and finger and I could see a big diamond ring flash.

He started toward me. I thought he was going to kick me, but I made it out of his way, stumbling up over the cans and bottles, and raced down the path.

Halfway down I could see the street and felt safer. I glanced back. The man had turned away and was walking toward the side street. The same long, black car stood at the curb. He got in and drove away.

Suddenly I felt all weak. My heart pounded so hard I thought I was having a heart attack. Then I knew it was just my weak stomach. I crept across the street holding my middle and threw up in the dark under a bush by the steps to my house. Then I started to shake.

I had to stop shaking, get my breath back, let my heart slow down. And I had to think.

Peewee

What was I going to tell Dad about that man? About how ugly he was? How he threw me on the ground and I thought he was going to kick me? The more I thought about it, the more chicken I felt. I'm fifteen and more than five feet five tall—not tall enough to be good at basketball but a lot taller than Woody. Even Woody couldn't have acted more chicken than I did. Why hadn't I used my head and sneaked around in the grass to get that monster's license number?

Besides not being too proud of the way I'd acted, I knew that if I ran into the house like a little kid and told Dad, he wouldn't let me go back there. He wanted me to get off the "music kick" anyhow. That would give him a good excuse. Scared as I was, I couldn't give up that room and all it meant to me. And just when everything was going so fine and we might get to play at the Poverty Palace!

Then I had another thought. What was that guy doing there? Feeling somewhat better, I hopped up. I was going to call Officer Bryant. I'd promised to do that if I saw anything out of line at Valentine's. This was worse than out of line.

After checking in with Mom, I closed off the room with the telephone in it and dialed the police. When they understood it was personal and important, I got to talk to Officer Bryant.

I gave him the whole story, even going back to tell him about the two gangster-type guys to whom Bob had spilled the beans. Officer Bryant gave me a hard time about that. "So Valentine wasn't just imagining things. If you'd leveled with me, you might not have had that run-in tonight. I'd have kept a closer watch on the place. The man you describe sounds like a bad-news type." He kept on quizzing me about what I'd seen around there. Then he asked, "And what kind of valuable stuff did Mr. Valentine leave in his house?" I said I didn't know unless it was furniture.

Then Officer Bryant sounded really serious. "Listen to me, Frank. I'm right worried about you. Promise me you won't go over there alone again. Reckon there's not much danger for five of you. But alone, that's different. You promise?"

I said, "Sure." And, man, did I feel a lot better!

Of course I told the guys the next day. We were already in our room and Woody got on me for not telling him before, so I soft-pedaled how scared I'd been. The rest of the group backed me up. If Officer Bryant said it was okay when we were all together, why worry?

Tracy asked Woody, "Suppose that man is waiting when we go out, what could he do?"

Woody said, "Well, I wouldn't hang around to find out. I'd be out on the street the quickest way."

"Okay," I said. "Then you can be the one to get his license number. I goofed on that."

Woody seemed even more scared, so Chester told him, "Be logical. Where else can we practice?"

Woody looked up at Bob, who was standing next to him and looking toward the boarded-up windows. We could hear a furniture van rumbling up the drive to Mrs. Merrifield's and sounds of workers over there. "The new family is moving in," Bob said. "We aren't all alone."

Woody brightened up. "Hey, that's right. Wonder who they are?"

I told them Mom had said their name was Rose, and that led into telling the rest of my parents' conversation. I even remembered to ask Chester about "Whispering."

That was why Chester looked so pleased when he came in late for practice on Thursday, followed by a skinny old guy. Chester grinned widely at me. "Hey, Frank, guess what. I've found someone who knows your song!" He looked back at the guy. "This is Peewee, fellows. Played with a band way back when. He knows 'Whispering.' "

Peewee was a washed-out kind of dim-looking character in a workingman's khakis. Long shreds of hair stuck over his bald spot. Chester handed him his fiddle, and, man! could Peewee ever play "Whispering"! I got what Mom meant—real sentimental corn.

We all tried it out. I picked away on the simple melody. Bob got it on the mandolin. Peewee led us all the time with the fiddle. We all worked on it until we were just beginning to get it into our heads. A few more times around and we'd have it.

Suddenly Peewee broke off and handed the fiddle back to Chester. "Gotta go," he said.

We were disappointed. "Where are you going?" we asked.

He looked at us as if we didn't know what was going on. "Gotta go to work."

"Okay," we said.

"Thanks for teaching us 'Whispering.' My mom will love it," I said. Then, just to be friendly, I asked, "Where do you work?"

He gave us that don't-you-know? look again. "Next door. For Mr. Rose." He eased toward the door. "I'll be back."

We watched him leave and asked Chester where he found him.

Chester jerked his thumb. "Out there on the sidewalk. He saw my fiddle case and started talking. I didn't know he worked next door."

"I wonder what he does," I said, ambling over to the window. The rest of the guys followed, looking for cracks in the boards where they could see through.

I found a knothole with a loose piece of wood in it and lifted it out with my handy-dandy Swiss army knife. Pee-wee and another guy were over there stringing up markers on the back lawn at Rose's. Someone I couldn't see seemed to be directing them because every now and then they stood up, looked the other way, and nodded their heads.

"They're putting in a pool," Bob announced.

"Must be an Olympic-sized pool if this is the end," Chester said. "How far back can he go?" He looked at me. "Do you know?"

I tried to think. "I can't remember anything but trees and bushes beyond the lawn—and that goes way back," I told him. Mom had sent me over with bridge tables one time when Mrs. Merrifield was having a party. I had set them up for her at the end of her huge living room with its sparkling crystal chandeliers. It opened onto the back lawn and I looked out at the old ladies, her aunts, sitting there.

No one was too excited about a swimming pool. They're all over the place in southern California. We drifted back to our instruments and started out with church songs. We played "Daniel Prayed," "Amazing Grace," and "Will the Circle Be Unbroken?" Bob started "Will the Circle Be Unbroken?" over and over again. Then we remembered "Orange Blossom Special." We'd gotten the message from Officer Bryant that this was one of the tunes that crossed the line from country music to bluegrass. We figured this one would be good for the Poverty Palace.

The next day was Friday and we were back in our room after school. Before we got started on anything else, Peewee drifted in. He'd brought his old fiddle, and we all worked on "Whispering" again.

When we'd learned that, we started on "Orange Blossom Special." Peewee tried keeping up with Chester's fiddling for a while, but then he got jittery. He trotted back and forth to the window, peeking through a crack in the boards. Suddenly he laid his fiddle down on the table and was gone like a shot.

We all stopped playing and listened. We heard the last faint hum from the motor of a powerful car that had gone into the garage at the Roses'.

It was Monday before we got back to practice, Peewee showed up again, and both of the other days we were there that week. We made it on Thursday, because by then we had enough nerve to go at night again. We planned to go Friday and Saturday nights and then at noon on Monday. That was Veterans Day. All five of us could be there to finish our practicing for the Poverty Palace. The contest was to be the following Sunday afternoon.

On Thursday Tracy got teed off about Peewee. He kept running to the window and peeking out the crack. "How come you're so scared Mr. Rose will catch you over here?"

Peewee gave Tracy a withering look. "Mr. Rose is the bossman."

"Bossman?" Tracy looked bewildered. "Bossman of what?"

"He's the bossman over there." Peewee jerked his elbow toward the Roses'. He started to go.

"Nice swimming pool he's building," Tracy said, not wanting Peewee to go away mad.

Peewee looked at him vacantly with his empty pale eyes. "Don't know nuthin' 'bout no swimmin' pool," he said flatly and dodged out the door.

We all looked after him. I scratched my head. Bob ran his fingers through his hair. Chester lowered his head looking through his glasses. Woody's eyebrows were down.

Tracy shook his head. His big baby face grinned around at us. Imitating Peewee, Tracy said, " 'Don't know nuthin' 'bout no swimmin' pool.' "

No one had the sense to look out and see what Peewee was talking about.

10

Tracy's Close Call

Everything went just fine Friday night. The Roses' place was all lighted up and we could hear cars swishing up the driveway. Remembering that beautiful living room, I knew they couldn't wait to show it off to their friends.

They must have a lot of friends, I thought, because cars were driving in again when we went back Saturday night. About noon that day, I'd seen Mr. Valentine's blue Porsche whizzing up his driveway. I was still worried that he might put a padlock on our door, so I felt relieved that night when the hasp was empty.

The guys pushed around in the dark as I unlocked the door and felt for the light. It wouldn't go on. "Bulb must be burned out," I told them. "We'll have to go back to my house and get another."

No one seemed to think too much about it. We'd gotten into a kind of hassle about what to play at the Poverty Palace. The manager had told us we could play only two numbers. "Orange Blossom Special" was a natural, but we each had our favorite for the second choice. I was hot on playing "Daybreak in Dixie." If any of those kids had ever tried to play banjo, they'd know how I'd perfected my picking on that. But Woody wanted to belt out a song, Chester wanted a fiddle tune, Bob could make "Uncle Pen" come to life on mandolin. We went around and around.

When we were in the kitchen at my house getting the light bulb, Woody's eyebrows were down. "Does your mom have any candles?" he asked.

"Sure," I said, pointing. "Over there, in the bottom drawer." Chester was talking, too. "Light bulbs last longer than a few weeks, don't they?"

Tracy's hand was on the refrigerator door. "Have you got any Cokes?"

"Sure, sure," I said. "Get one for each of us."

"Where are the matches?" Woody asked.

I told him and Bob cleared his throat, so that we all looked up at him. "Mr. Valentine could be saving electricity. Maybe he turned the power off."

"Could be; he was over there today," I told him.

Bob must have been right because the new bulb didn't work. Chester had brought over a big box of kitchen matches and struck one while I tried the bulb. Then, when it had burned down almost to his finger, he dropped it, and one of the newspapers on our table caught fire. We stomped it out and that was why we wadded the rest of them all up, throwing them into the corner after we lighted our candle.

We stood the candle in an empty Coke bottle in the middle of the table. Maybe we were a little tense because we laughed a lot as we played one tune after another.

Chester was across from me. The light from the candle

flashed on his glasses, and his alive-looking hair flipped over his forehead as he fiddled. The huge shadow moving behind him was eerie. We all had our regular spots by the table, with Bob at the end. In that dim room I guess we all looked pretty spooky. And the whole setup was spooky, I had to admit. What was Mr. Valentine up to? Who was that monster who knocked me down? Having no real light somehow scared me.

Veterans Day I gave the guys the key because I was late getting back from playing basketball. They went on ahead to our room while I had a quick lunch. I searched the refrigerator, eating what I could find. Then I grabbed an apple and my banjo and rushed over there.

Before I was in sight of the patio, I smelled something funny. Then I saw the guys come stumbling out of our room in a cloud of evil-smelling smoke. All but Tracy!

The guys were coughing, rubbing their eyes, and looking dazed. "Where's Tracy?" I yelled. More smoke was streaming out the door. "Where's Tracy?" I screamed again.

I ran up and shook Bob. He couldn't stop coughing but he turned and started toward our room, pointing his finger.

Just then, Peewee, dragging a hose, rushed through the bushes. He darted around the group to a faucet while I charged toward the door of our room.

At school, I'd heard a lecture on fires, so I took a big breath before I started in, crouched down as low as I could, and barged ahead. Even with my eyes closed I figured I knew that room by heart. My breath should last one run around our table and Tracy had to be near it with his bass, so that I couldn't miss him.

I felt the table with my hand as I ran around, but I began to think my breath wouldn't last. I felt as if I were going to burst when a stream of cold water struck me full in the face. Gasping for breath, the water went up my nose and, half knocked out, I fell down. What I fell on made a deep, hollow sound. Tracy's bass!

That jolted me. I tried to get up, but I was under the table. I couldn't see a thing, but even with coughing, I felt around by the bass and found Tracy's leg.

The water was splashing off the top of the table and I could tell by the sound which way the door was. I pulled that big lug Tracy halfway to the door when the water must have hit him and he jerked up.

He didn't know what he was doing and started back into the room. I didn't even think. I just slugged him in the jaw, grabbed his leg, and kept on hauling him to the door.

From then on everything was just a jumble. I remember seeing Bob and Chester carrying Tracy into the middle of the patio. I couldn't see Woody, but Peewee stood in the door to our room with the hose. No more smoke was coming out.

I just kept stumbling around in the cans, bottles, and dry leaves in the patio, feeling lousy. Finally Tracy came to, with Chester and Bob kneeling beside him. My stomach hurt, and I was sick all over the cans and junk. Bob jumped up, held my head and mopped my face with his handkerchief. Then I heard sirens and saw Peewee take off like a shot.

I was feeling well enough to head back into the room to get Tracy's bass. Instead Bob got it for me. Tracy struggled to his feet and we started hauling the bass to my house. Halfway down the path we met Woody. He'd called the fire department, so he had to be there when they came.

The rest of us made it to the curb just as Officer Bryant pulled up on his motorcycle.

He took one look at Tracy's bloodless face and soggy clothes, stopped his bike, and hopped off. Mom wasn't home, so he told us what to do for Tracy.

We already knew what to do; we'd all taken first aid in Scouts. After we got his wet clothes off and covered him up in my bed, Chester made him some instant coffee. Tracy didn't like it much, but it kind of jolted him. He began to look human again.

I got out of my wet clothes and into my bathrobe and stretched out in my comfortable chair, the one Gramps gave me. Bob and Chester were telling what happened. Smoke had been coming from the newspapers and lumber in the corner of our room. Thinking it would be easy to put out by scattering the stuff, they went to work. Instead of going out, the whole pile of junk flared up in their faces. They realized they were in trouble and panicked, pushing Tracy out before he could get his bass. He'd gone back in.

"Yeah, I know," I said, rubbing my swelling knuckles.

Tracy's head was on my pillow. He felt his jaw. "I wondered how I hurt my jaw. You had to slug me to . . ." He managed a half-smile. "Thanks."

We'd heard the fire department come clanging, sirens wailing, to a stop, while we took care of Tracy. Bob had taken up a watch at my window. "Mr. Valentine's been up there," he said. "Now he's driving up the Roses' drive."

Chester had brought up some furniture polish to work on Tracy's bass. He finished and went to watch with Bob. "The firemen are leaving and Woody is coming back," he announced.

In no time we could hear Woody running up the stairs.

He puffed in, all out of breath. "Let me tell you—" He paused to catch his breath. "At first the fire department tried to blame it on us!" He scowled and sat down on the end of my bed. "Guess they still do, kind of, because we left those matches over there." He glanced around at the group. "Man! Was I glad Officer Bryant showed up. He told them we were authorized to be there and got Mr. Valentine to come down to prove it." Woody's eyebrows went up in a big grin. "Mr. Valentine recognized me right away. He said, 'This is the guitar player in the group who uses this room.' He even thanked me for turning in the alarm. Then the firemen decided that rats could easily have ignited those stick matches and started a fire in all that trash."

"Oh yeah, sure," said Chester. "The matches were on the table. The junk was way across the room."

I didn't believe rats had started that fire, unless they were human rats. And in spite of all the nice things Mr. Valentine had done for us, I didn't trust him. Maybe we were bait in a trap. Just by luck Tracy hadn't been asphyxiated.

The Poverty Palace

We wouldn't have gone back to our room that week except that we'd finally decided to play "Black-Eyed Susy" for our other tune. The singing is tricky, but we thought with Woody's good voice we could show how versatile the group was. One good practice would do it, so we all hurried over after school.

What a sour, evil smell! All that was left of the lumber was charred black. The plaster hung down brown and soggy from the smoke and water. Streaks of dampness showed on the floor. We left the door open so the room could dry out better and also because we hoped Peewee would come in. We wanted to thank him for putting out the fire.

After we'd practiced a while and Peewee didn't show up, I pried the plug out of the knothole with my knife and looked out. I nearly went through the floor with what I saw. "Will you look at this!" I yelled.

69

The rest of the guys rushed over and climbed around to find places to look out.

"Some swimming pool!" Tracy yelled. Instead of a swimming pool the whole yard as far as we could see was covered with blacktop. "That's parking enough for a whole supermarket!"

But the parking lot wasn't what I was looking at. Peewee and the bad-news monster who'd given me the scare were walking around, pacing off the blacktop. I began to shake. "That man! You guys see that man with Peewee? He's the one I told you about!" He looked just the same—as ugly as before.

Woody turned to me. He was shaking too. "Look at how big he is!"

Even in broad daylight the guy looked evil. He was dressed the same as the other night, in a white shirt and trousers up to his armpits. His ring flashed as he waved his cigar, directing Peewee.

"No wonder Peewee's so scared," Chester said. "That's got to be Mr. Rose."

"And we've been feeling so cozy over here with our new neighbors," Woody said, scowling. "If I'd known—"

"Peewee and Mr. Rose don't live in that big place all alone," Bob said. "There's got to be a Mrs. Rose. All those cars—"

"Sure," Tracy agreed. "Mrs. Rose is probably a nice, friendly woman. They have lots of friends. Two nights they had parties."

We thought about that and even I knew it made sense. But not Woody. "I don't care." He started toward the door. "I'm leaving. Too many screwy things are going on around here."

"Oh, come on," Tracy said. "We're okay. Officer Bryant said so, and you just talked to Mr. Valentine."

Woody hesitated. Chester pulled Woody back, saying, "Just wait until we finish off practicing 'Black-Eyed Susy.' You're going to win the contest for us singing at the Poverty Palace."

Woody half smiled and started us off with his guitar. "Aw, I was just kidding," he said, and I knew it was because Tracy reminded Woody of Mr. Valentine. Hearing Mr. Valentine tell the whole fire department that Woody was the guitar player in the band had built up his ego. He worked hard at "Black-Eyed Susy," and in an unexpected way that led to complications at the Poverty Palace.

But the Poverty Palace was a blast. They have what they call a theater room, with little tables and seats for quite a few. It was packed. We didn't catch on to how packed it was until later. It was really a Sunday afternoon kiddie show with all ages of kids, so we were glad we'd planned to play "Orange Blossom Special" with its choo-choo-train sounds.

We didn't have the problem about tuning that we'd had at assembly. There was a door marked "Performers," and we were told to wait there. And there was a little room next to it that I figured must be soundproof, for we took turns with the other groups tuning in there.

We found out we were going to be judged by applause and by a regular professional group that was billed for the week.

The Flanigan kid, Kevin, and his group were there to play too. They called themselves the Smoky Mountain Boys and were dressed up in cowboy hats and flashy vests. Two guys had electric guitars. Man! With that kind of taste was I glad we beat them out!

We didn't win, but we were in the finals, and the kids seemed to like us a lot. The group that won had the audience packed with their friends. We hadn't told any of ours to come, so we felt good to have placed second.

But we didn't feel so good about what happened out in the alley afterward. The Poverty Palace is on an alley behind some buildings. All the audience had gone and the rest of us got out there ahead of Woody.

Then the Flanigan kid's group, the Smoky Mountain Boys, in their fancy vests and cowboy hats came out. Woody was in their midst. They were all talking to him at once, and we heard him shout, "Nope!" He swung his guitar case ahead of him and tried to break out of the group. But they closed in on him even closer, so we couldn't see him at all. They were talking to him harder and faster.

Tracy pushed his bass at me and he and Bob went over to help Woody.

One of the Smoky Mountain Boys, a five-by-five football type, squared off at Tracy. It looked as if we were in for a fight. I leaned the bass up against the building just as that kid looked up at Bob.

Bob's eyes seemed to spark with rage. His hair stood up as if it were electric. His voice turned into a roar. "What's coming off here!"

While they all stared up at Bob, Tracy pushed in and made way for Woody to squeeze out. The Smoky Mountain Boys closed the gaps around Bob and Tracy just as Chester and I moved up in back. We heard Kevin Flanigan tell Bob, "We only wanted to make a deal with your guitar player." He sounded apologetic.

"What kind of deal?" Bob growled, bending down to look him in the eye.

Two of the group disappeared to get their instruments. "Aw, just a deal," Kevin said. "He'll tell you about it."

Tracy wasn't going to let them off so easy. "Woody doesn't want any part of your crummy group!"

"Crummy, huh?" the five-by-five guy said. "If we'd had your guy on electric guitar, we'd have beat you out!"

"Oh yeah!" Tracy yelled.

There was some more jawing and the big kid shouted, "Yeah! You guys think you're so smart. Just wait! We'll show you!"

Bob yanked Tracy away before they could tangle and we all marched out to the street to wait for Mom.

Before Mom got there to pick us up, Officer Bryant rode up on his bike. "How'd you do?" he asked. "If I hadn't been on duty, I'd have looked in."

"We did okay," I said. "We came in second."

He grinned. "Very good!" Then he turned to Tracy. "How are you feeling? You sure look different from the way you did after the fire."

"I'm okay," Tracy told him. "But I wouldn't want to go through that again."

"Well, I reckon not," Officer Bryant said. "I was right worried. But I guess things will be okay over there now. Mr. Valentine told me there's no longer cause to worry."

Mom drove up just then, so we couldn't tell Officer Bryant that the bad-news guy was really Mr. Rose, our new neighbor.

12

The Smoky Mountain Boys

On the way home from the Poverty Palace Mom asked us if we would play for the party her hospital guild was going to have at our house in January. Just a few numbers, she said, while the dance band took its break. That was one reason why we went back to our room the very next day, Monday. We planned to run through "Whispering" again, and we'd picked up some ideas at the Poverty Palace.

We didn't get to do much practicing, though. The weather had turned cold with rain. Another poor little bird had flown in and, seeming half dead, fluttered helplessly around until we caught it, warmed it in our hands, and carried it out. We put it under some thick bushes to stay dry and it hopped away okay.

Then we started talking about boarding up the windows a little better to keep birds out. But if we did that, the room would be too smelly. We began to haul the sour, charred boards out and Peewee turned up to help us.

None of the boards seemed good enough for closing up the tops of the windows.

When Peewee learned what we wanted to do, he got a sort of a light in his eyes. He went over to the Roses' and brought back boards and a ladder, closing us in from outside.

I heard Tracy talking to him while he was working. "Is it okay for you to bring that stuff over here?" he asked. "Won't Mrs. Rose want you to use that lumber for something?"

I couldn't see Peewee, but there was a pause, so I knew he was giving that don't-you-know? look of his. "Mrs. Rose is no good. She went off."

"You mean," Tracy went on, "you mean just you and Mr. Rose live over there?"

Peewee clammed up. I could hear him pounding nails furiously. When he had finished he took off without even coming in to help us with "Whispering."

Woody had heard Tracy and Peewee, too. "Sure, sure," he said when Peewee had gone and we were all in our room ready to tune. " 'Mrs. Rose must be a nice friendly woman!' " After explaining to Chester and Bob, he said, "This is the craziest neighborhood going!" He scowled at me.

I threw out my hands. "Don't blame me! We're one hundred percent normal over at my house. I don't know what's coming off any more than you do." I held out the key to Woody. "If you think something's fishy, lock us in." I looked around at the guys. "What do you say? Has having this room been fun, or hasn't it?"

They all yelled, "Yeah!" And Tracy snuggled up to his

bass, beaming his big baby face around at us. "How lucky can a bunch of guys get!"

With nearly getting asphyxiated in the fire, I thought that was pretty much for Tracy to say. But I was the one who was wrong. I shouldn't have rallied the group together that way.

Woody pretended to shake again and locked us in. "The best way I know to stay lucky is to be careful." Then he came back, picked up his guitar, and started on the song he'd learned from Officer Bryant, the one about Amelia Earhart. When Woody lays one on like that, he really gets to you.

We all went for it and told him so. That's what bluegrass means to us—what Officer Bryant told us about—a sort of old-time back-porch closeness that is solid and like our name: indestructible. I felt all good and cozy and comfortable inside again. All of us must feel it when we're playing, or how else could we know just what note to pick next? But there's no need to talk about it.

We were really far out playing, learning our parts to back up Woody's singing "Amelia Earhart" when, boom! boom! boom! The entire room seemed to shake.

The sound came from just outside, and the whole group piled up against our door, rattling the handle to get out. Woody had to push through us with the key. When we made it outside, there was a handful of smoking cherry bombs mixed in with the cans and bottles of the patio. Not a soul was in sight!

We dashed around, even running down our path to the street and Chester, adding it up as usual, said, "Those Smoky Mountain Boys! Talk about rotten losers!"

I had to agree. There might be strange people around, but cherry bombs? That was kid stuff. I couldn't imagine Mr. Valentine or Mr. Rose shooting off cherry bombs. And, of course, the Flanigans were only two blocks away and Mrs. Flanigan had told us where to get the bass. The Smoky Mountain Boys were sure to know we were using the room. "I'll tell you what I'll do," I told the guys. "Curtis is my friend. I'll ask him. If it's those guys, we'll go over and cream them."

But, after that, we didn't get back to our room for quite a while. Thanksgiving came along and during that long weekend Bob went to Canada to visit his cousin. Then came a day that changed everything.

13

Our Bob

I'd been down playing basketball that day when everything changed. I could tell something was wrong the way Mom looked at me when I came home. She was waiting at the door.

"Frank," she said and gulped. Mom almost never cries, but big tears crowded out of her eyes, forming glistening paths down her cheeks. "I've got some terrible news for you."

I thought of Gramps and everyone but who it really was.

"It's Bob. Your Bob." She struggled to speak and pushed her fists into her eyes the way a baby does. "He—he was killed in an automobile accident."

For a second I just stood there—in shock, I guess. Then my whole insides seemed to fall away. I thought, even hoped, Mom would stretch out her arms and let me come and cry like a little kid. Instead I found myself putting an arm around her and leading her to a sofa. The tears were all there in the back of my head, but they came much later, when I was alone.

"Tell me about it," I heard myself say.

She huddled in a corner of the sofa and told me. Bob's sister had called. Bob and his cousin in Canada had both been killed. The cousin had been taking Bob for a ride in his new car when a truck hit them. Mom tried to get up.

I felt unreal. A part of my head didn't work right for a long time after that. "Where are you going?" I asked.

"To see Bob's parents," she said. "Wash your face and I'll wash mine."

I helped her up.

There were several cars on the pleasant tree-shaded street in front of the Nortons' house. It was as if we were expected. No one said anything about Bob, but Mom went up to Mrs. Norton sitting there with some other ladies and embraced and kissed her, so I did the same. She was a nice lady—always good to us kids.

Then I shook hands with Bob's dad, Charley. He was our Boy Scout leader and I knew him well. Pretty soon Chester, Woody, and Tracy were there, all Bob's best friends. Charley got us together and took us out back.

"I want to show you what we just did out here by the pool," he said.

Off the back of their nice white colonial house was a whole new place to sit and overlook the pool. I didn't really like all that new part stuck on there, but I wanted to please Charley so I looked around for sincere things to say. He talked and talked about the deck—the kind of lumber, the workmen, how much it cost. I knew, we all knew, that he was leading up to something, and that just for a while he didn't want to think about what had hap-

pened. He needed to have us around him and we wanted
to be there. So we asked him questions. We told him how
good it looked.

We had hung around with Charley like this many times
before waiting for Bob, who was always late. And this
time the door banged just the way it would if Bob were
coming out but, of course, it wasn't Bob. It was a lady
bringing Charley a drink. He took a sip and put it down
and said what I suspected he had brought us outside to
say.

"Ned," that's Bob's brother, "will be one of the pallbearers. Bob," his voice faltered momentarily, "would want
you."

"Sure," we said, "anything." We didn't know exactly
what pallbearers did, but we figured we could find out. If
Mr. Norton thought we could do anything to help, we
wanted to do it.

I hated to leave him when Mom came and said it was
time to go. When she kissed Charley good-bye, I said,
"See you guys later."

They knew what I meant, and pretty soon Tracy, Woody,
and Chester were with me up in my room, with the snot
flying along with all the cuss words we knew. After a while
I had a kind of feeling that Bob was there, too. I sat
back in my comfortable chair and heard him say, "Errgh!"
Right away I knew what he wanted. The guys had all
quieted down and I looked at each of them. It was as if we
all got the message at the same time.

"What Bob would like," Chester said, "is our music."

All we had there was my banjo, but we sang all the
church songs we knew. We started and ended with "Will
the Circle Be Unbroken?" We also sang, played, and

hummed "Daniel Prayed," "Amazing Grace," and "All the Good Times Are Past and Gone."

Then we just sat there for a long time. Suddenly Woody's eyebrows came up. "In my church they sometimes use guitars to back up the choir."

"They had a man sing hymns at my grandfather's funeral," Tracy said. "And those songs . . ." Tracy's big baby-face puddled up.

We gazed at him. The rest of us hadn't been to a funeral.

"Our songs are just like hymns," Chester said.

"Bob's mom sings in the choir," I said. "Maybe I should call her and ask if they would be okay."

"Go ahead," the other guys said. "Call her."

I did. And though she had seemed so cool when everyone was there kissing her, I could hear the tears. At last she said, "My friends in the church choir want to sing for the service. But after the b-burial most of the people who are close to us will come here. If you would like to play then . . ." Her voice fell off and I knew she was crying.

"We will be there," I said.

We kind of got ourselves together after that. We felt the funeral wouldn't really say anything to us about our Bob. We all had had religious training of one kind or another, but we couldn't give him up. Bob would always be there with us, even if we couldn't see him.

The funeral was grim. Lots of people came, even Officer Bryant. We had to carry the casket in and sit in the front pew. We had been instructed, but we still had to watch Ned and the three older men who were pallbearers to know what to do. Never, never, as long as I live, will I forget how awful it was, carrying Bob. Light as he seemed, the casket was heavy—very heavy.

The funeral cortege went down the pleasant tree-shaded street where Bob lived—or had lived. When we got back there after lifting the casket out by the grave, we felt nearly dead, too. We went inside the house. It was filled with people and they had food—cakes, baked ham, casseroles. We couldn't stay in there. At last we got it together under a tree on the front lawn. Very softly we played. Over and over we came back to "Will the Circle Be Unbroken?" At the last we drifted off into "Uncle Pen," Bob's other favorite. It shouldn't have had much tune without Bob's mandolin, but I glanced at the guys and I knew they were hearing what I did—Bob playing the high mandolin part.

14

Togetherness

For weeks we went to our room every day after school.
We had to get together—together with Bob.

You wouldn't think an old boarded-up room with the
plaster hanging down could seem like a church. But it did.
It was dim and quiet and seemed to have a holy feeling.

First, Woody would light the candle. Then we would
take our places around the table and tune up. As we began
to play "Will the Circle Be Unbroken?" very softly, we
watched Bob's place. I could see him gradually take shape
in the familiar pose, his blond head tilted to watch his
fingering, and the sweet high notes came into my head
to blend into the sounds of our instruments. In a little while
we would drift into "Amazing Grace" and on through the
other church music we knew. Sometimes Peewee would
wander in and in a bewildered way stand next to Chester
and follow his fiddling.

After a few weeks of this, Charley, Bob's father, gave

us Bob's mandolin, and we told Officer Bryant about it. He seemed to know that we went to our room from school every day because he said, "I'll stop by on my day off and show you how we play mandolin down in Swain County."

Woody and I made room for him on our side of the table, so he wouldn't take Bob's place. His quick eyes darted around to each of our faces as, without speaking, we went through our ritual of lighting the candle and tuning. Then he took Bob's mandolin out of its case and tuned it, too. When we started playing, I concentrated on Bob's place and he seemed to be there, maybe dimmer and with a lighter feeling about him, but that may have been the way Officer Bryant was playing his mandolin. We sang all the church songs, enjoying that great high tenor voice of Officer Bryant.

He stopped us after "All the Good Times Are Past and Gone" and made it into a question, "All the good times are past and gone?"

We looked at Bob's place to find the answer and I guess they all heard what I did, Bob croaking, "Errgh! Come on, you guys! How about a little good old corn?"

Chester started first on his fiddle, and before we knew it we were laying into "Old Joe Clark" a hundred miles an hour, with Officer Bryant moving us on from verse to verse. We went from that to "Salty Dog" and "Hot Corn, Cold Corn" until we were all gasping for breath and falling off in our playing. At last Officer Bryant laid Bob's mandolin on the table and clapped. We were relaxed for the first time in weeks. And still I knew Bob was right there with us.

Even when Christmas vacation came we went to our room religiously but we did a lot of other things too. Chester's father decided we were so good he just had to tape us. Tracy's brother took us across town to play for his fraternity. My parents, for the first time, asked us to play for them and really listened. They were all very kind trying to help us forget Bob. But we didn't forget him.

We were acting more normal, though, and decided to have a birthday party for Woody just after Christmas. I told Mom, and I guess she was glad we were going to have a party because she turned me loose in the supermarket to buy stuff. She even gave me money for a cake for Woody. That was when I ran into Curtis Flanigan, who was wheeling a shopping cart.

"Hey, Curt!" I said. I hadn't seen him since the cherry bombs and I remembered I had told the guys I would nail him.

Curtis said, "Hey, Frank!" and gave me that old friendly grin of his.

I hated to get after him about his brother, but I'd promised the guys. "What's with that brother of yours?"

He looked at me as if I had lost my marbles. Then the light seemed to dawn. He grinned, "Oh, you mean way back when your band and the Smoky Mountain Boys played at the Poverty Palace?"

I nodded.

"They said your group was great. They needed a guitar player and asked your guy—that what you mean?"

"Yeah." I could see he didn't know about the cherry bombs and I didn't want to tell him about our room at Mr. Valentine's if he didn't already know. "They told Woody they had a job playing for money. How about that? Trying to buy our guitar player."

"Aw, that was just a deal my mom cooked up." Curt passed it off. "No big thing. But the Smoky Mountain Boys are pretty good." The Flanigans stick together.

"They fake it too much for us," I told him. "With those hokey vests, hats, and electric guitars." Then I felt sorry because Curtis looked puzzled. "How's your Chevy coming?" I asked. He likes cars.

Curtis grinned again. "I was going great until I ran out of parts," he said. "Know where I can get a carburetor?"

"Tracy's brother might have one. He had a Chevy he was working on for a while. Then he went over to law school. His mom is always fussing about all that junk out there. I'll ask Tracy."

"Great!" Curtis said, pushing off with his cart. "See you."

Funny, before Curtis got interested in cars and I got interested in bluegrass, we had a lot in common.

But I didn't worry about Curtis too much. The guys drifted into my room to listen to an old record of the Greenbriar Boys Chester had found. After that we went down to the kitchen to load Tracy up with the stuff for the party because his bass was in our room and he didn't have an instrument to carry.

Mom came in to tell us to be sure to get back by ten. "Your neighbors, the Roses, seem to be having another party," she told us. "This is party season—they've had one every night for weeks. Guess you won't disturb them." She caught a bag of potato chips that was slipping off Tracy's load and handed it to Chester as we took off. "Just don't forget about our party—the guild party. That's this next Saturday."

We told her we wouldn't and by now, for no good reason, we were feeling sort of kooky. We took our time wandering down the dark street in front of my house. What with losing Bob and all the other things going on, we hadn't been worrying about Mr. Valentine and Mr. Rose. I guess that was why we had a fresh, relaxed viewpoint. We came up with an idea to explain Mr. Rose.

15

Movie People

We fooled around out there on the dark sidewalk in front of my house, checking out the Continentals, Rolls-Royces, Cadillacs, and Mercedes going into the tunnel of trees up to Mr. Rose's parking lot. Sometimes there would be three cars waiting to make the turn.

"Man," Tracy observed. "He must be putting on some spread there."

"He has to be some kind of multimillionaire to entertain all those people every night," Chester decided.

In the cars the men were dressed in dark suits and the women wore evening wraps. A glittering low-slung Jaguar pulled into line.

"Now, there's my kind of car," Tracy said.

"I like Porsches better," Chester told him.

Woody was peering at the people in the Jag. "Will you look at that! See? That's Sylvia Maars! I'm sure, I just saw her new picture, *Atonement*."

A spectacular blonde holding a long cigarette holder

rested against her white furs. It was Sylvia Maars, all right. No one could mistake her.

We stood there gawking and Chester said, "Got it! Mr. Rose—maybe he's a movie mogul!"

"Hey!" We looked at one another. Why hadn't we thought of that before? Hollywood's not that far by freeway. People who work in the studios live all over town.

Even Mr. Rose being so ugly made sense. Peewee called him the bossman. Big-shot movie people are supposed to be tyrants. They don't like having kids interfering with their private lives. That could be why he gave me such a bad time.

I was trying to add this up in my mind when a motorcycle policeman pulled up on the curb side of the Jag. Instantly Sylvia Maars leaned to whisper to the man driving. She waved her cigarette holder toward the street and the Jag flashed around the cars in line and sped off. The other cars disappeared up the drive, leaving the cop at the curb. We saw it was Officer Bryant.

He called to us to go on up the side street and roared ahead. When we got to the path, he was waiting. "How are things going?" he asked. He looked at Tracy's load of Cokes and things and grinned. "Appears to me they're going pretty good. You're going to have a party."

"Yeah," Tracy said. "But we don't have the class of the one next door. Did you see Sylvia Maars in that Jag?"

"It looked like Sylvia Maars," Officer Bryant said. "I wasn't sure. They took off as I pulled up."

"Chester figured out who Mr. Rose is," I told Officer Bryant. "A movie mogul." Then I remembered I hadn't told him that he was the same man who'd given me the scare the other night. I told him about that and the guys told about the swimming pool that had turned into a parking lot.

Tracy said, "Having a party every night. I guess he needs it."

"Every night?" Officer Bryant stared at him. "I reckon you're kidding."

"That's what Frank's mom told us."

Officer Bryant looked questioningly at the rest of us.

"That's what she said," we agreed.

He pushed up the strap and took off his helmet to scratch behind his ear. "Hmm." He looked past Mr. Valentine's toward Mr. Rose's. Then he slammed his helmet back on, jumped on the starting pedal, and roared off without another word.

We ambled up the path talking and laughing about Sylvia Maars and about how dumb we'd been not guessing any sooner who Mr. Rose was. I was trying to believe it. I didn't want anything to stop us from getting together with Bob.

When we got to our room, I fished out the key and the others crowded around me. Tracy complained, "Hurry it up, will you? This stuff is getting heavy!" when whoosh! a bucket of water poured over us and a yellow plastic pail bounced off Chester's head. That is, we saw it was a yellow plastic pail after the panic was over. We didn't know what hit us at first. The others milled around until Woody got the candle lighted.

Chester had gotten it worst. He took off his glasses and held his head down to shake the water out of his hair. "Something tells me we aren't welcome here." His voice came out high and squeaky, the way it does sometimes.

"No kidding, whatever gave you that idea?" Tracy said.

Woody felt the sleeve of his T-shirt. He took it off, twisted the water out of the sleeve, and held it by the candle to dry.

Chester was running his fingers through his wet hair and patting the spot where the bucket had hit. He didn't seem to think it was much of a joke.

"You aren't hurt, are you?" I asked.

"Nope—just mad!" He wiped off his glasses and growled. "Those Smoky Mountain Boys!" His hands reached out to wring an imaginary neck.

"Hey!" I remembered. "I forgot to tell you. If they are after us, Curtis doesn't know anything about it." I told them all he had said to me in the supermarket. We were sitting in our places on the edge of the table. In the candle's glow I could see all their faces. They looked damp and upset but not puzzled, the way I felt.

Tracy opened the potato chips and started eating. "I've never had any idea about what my brother was up to. Why should Curtis?"

Chester agreed. Woody turned his T-shirt by the candle to dry the other side of the sleeve. I guess I must still have had fur in my brain because I didn't say anything. I just slipped around in back of Woody to open the cake box and light the candles. He pretended not to notice until the cake was in front of him and we began singing "Happy Birthday." Chester grabbed his fiddle, swaying to his elaborate accompaniment as his wet hair flipped around wildly. Before Woody could blow out his candles, Chester shifted into "Will the Circle Be Unbroken?" and I watched the guys' heads turn toward Bob's place at the table.

Then I did something I've never been able to account for. Bob's mandolin case was lying there next to Peewee's fiddle. I opened it, took out his instrument, and tuned for a second. I played "Happy Birthday" with all the frills just as if I'd been playing mandolin for years.

We left a big mess and Chester and I went back the next day to clean it up. You wouldn't have believed how glad Peewee was to see us. He hadn't been around for about a week. Peewee came through the bushes next door all filled with joy. Then he saw we didn't have our instruments and his face fell a mile.

"Why you over here if you're not going to play?" he asked.

"Oh, we left some junk when we were here last night," Chester told him.

Peewee tagged along in as we gathered up the stuff. He picked up his old fiddle and tuned up. He played an ancient jazz number. We asked him what it was. He said it was "Mississippi Mud." So he played it again and sang some hokey words. We liked the tune but we didn't like the words. We knew he was trying to con us into having him teach it to the group, so we just passed it off by asking him to play something else. We sat on the table and ate popcorn and listened to Peewee fiddle his heart out.

Suddenly he stopped in a sort of panic. "The bossman come back?"

We shrugged—how would we know?

Laying down his fiddle and bow very gently next to Bob's mandolin case, he took off. We followed him out, carrying our stuff, and locked up. We'd already started down the path when Peewee came jogging along after us.

"I seen some lights," he announced.

"What do you mean?" Chester asked him.

"I seen some lights there." He jerked his thumb back toward Mr. Valentine's house. Then, seeing we were unimpressed, he went on, "Guy what owns your house is loco." He tapped the side of his head.

Chester looked at me. I could see he was wondering what Peewee knew about Mr. Valentine. He tried to find out. Taking off his glasses, he grinned at Peewee. "Oh, come on, fellow, Mr. Valentine isn't loco."

But Peewee just gave us his don't-you-know? look. Then his pale eyes got a kind of desperate look in them. "I seen some lights," he repeated. "Y'all better stay away at night."

Chester looked at me. There was no doubt of Peewee's sincerity. "Thank you for telling us," Chester said. "We'll be careful."

Peewee didn't answer. His eyes were glued on Mr. Rose's shrubbery. We looked, too. There was a gleam of light as Mr. Rose's car drove in. Peewee was off like a shot.

Chester and I wandered on down the path asking each other what Peewee had been talking about.

16

Questions

When we went back after school on Tuesday, I decided to look for clues to what Peewee had been talking about. I inspected the padlocked door on the other side of the patio. Near it was a yellow piece of cardboard like the flap from a film folder. Chester was watching me and I handed it to him. It looked new—not like the rest of the old junk out there. Then I unlocked the door to our room. The place was a shambles.

All the plaster on the ceiling seemed to have fallen into the room. Tracy let out a howl and rushed over to his bass. It had been standing upright, leaning against his end of our table. Now it lay half buried in plaster. Our table was a powdery gray mountain.

"Bob's mandolin!" I yelled and began digging.

Chester dug, too. "Peewee's fiddle!"

Woody helped in the suffocating cloud of gritty plaster dust that rose around us.

Almost right away Tracy gave a happy yelp. "She's okay! She's okay!"

Then we found Bob's mandolin, which had been protected by its case, and the broken Coke bottle and candle. Even without choking from the dust I was feeling a little sick remembering the gentle way Peewee had laid his fiddle there with the bow beside it. With each heavy piece of plaster we lifted off, I felt more sure it had been smashed.

Chester found the sad little heap of dusty dark wood. He held it up by its neck to show us its crazy dangling strings and with the other hand slipped off his glasses. He shook his head sorrowfully. "Poor old Peewee!"

We all stood around feeling miserable. Woody began to sneeze and someone said, "Let's get out of this dust!"

I put Bob's mandolin by the door with my banjo to take home and Tracy hauled the bass outside. Then we all just stood around feeling sunk.

Unexpectedly it was Woody who cheered us up. "Well, now it's down. I won't have to worry about that anymore."

"Yeah?" we said in surprise. "What do you mean?"

Woody's eyebrows were up. "Why—the ceiling. I knew it was coming down any time. But you guys are always giving me a hard time. I didn't want to say anything."

Chester stared at him. "You don't think someone did it?"

Woody shrugged. "How could they do it? It just fell, that's all."

"What about if someone was walking around in the room upstairs?" I asked, remembering Peewee's far-out talk.

All of us looked at the upstairs windows. They were intact on that side—just covered with dust and cobwebs.

"Could be," Woody said. "But it was ready to come down anyhow."

That was a load off our minds. Maybe this wasn't part of the plot to get us out of our room after all.

Tracy had found an old piece of cloth in the rubbish and was dusting off his bass. Then he started tuning, listening closely. "Well," he said, as casually as if nothing had happened, "let's get started."

"In that mess?" asked Chester. Then he turned to me. "Frank, how about borrowing some shovels and brooms from your house?"

"Why, sure."

It didn't take us too long with all of us working. We just dumped it all out in the patio with the rest of the trash. We brought over some Cokes, so we'd have a bottle to hold our candle and a box to hold the bits of Peewee's fiddle.

Mom was in the kitchen when we returned the brooms. She was pretty upset when she found out the ceiling had fallen down. "Thank goodness it didn't fall when you were there," she said. Then she smiled at us. "It's a wonder it didn't. You boys really do shake the rafters. That reminds me—what are you going to play for our party?"

We told her, but Mom wasn't really interested in what we planned to play. She wouldn't have known most of the titles anyway.

We went back for our secret meetings with Bob every day that week. We would have called that enough, but Officer Bryant left word with Mom that he would meet us at Mr. Valentine's Friday night.

The cars were coming up Mr. Rose's driveway and it was about nine o'clock when Officer Bryant barged in. He was dressed like us again, and carrying his guitar case. We stopped right in the middle of "Fisher's Hornpipe"— our ritual with Bob was over and we could hear his mandolin come in, as it always had. We sat or stood in our places at the table, with the candle in the middle making our big shadows wave wildly against the walls.

Officer Bryant looked us over. He scratched behind his ear. "What are you practicing for—Halloween? Why don't you turn on the light?"

We told him about the light, the cherry bombs, and getting booby-trapped with the water.

"But nothing has happened lately," Tracy told him. "Except that the ceiling fell down."

With Officer Bryant there, everything that had happpened began to seem a little funny. We grinned at him and he grinned back, looking up at the laths and joists overhead with chunks of plaster still clinging to them. Then his grin faded. He shook his head and worry lines came into his face. "Why didn't you boys tell me about all this? Mr. Valentine made me responsible for reporting anything out of line that happened. I'm right disappointed in you."

He was looking straight at me, making me realize how much we hadn't told him. But before I could say anything the rest of the guys were explaining.

"We think it was the Smoky Mountain Boys," Tracy told him. "They're the group we beat at the Poverty Palace."

"Silly stuff like cherry bombs and water-bagging didn't hurt Mr. Valentine's place," Chester said.

"And the ceiling was ready to come down from the first day we played here," Woody added. "The only damage it did was to Peewee's fiddle."

"Poor old Peewee," Chester said. "It smashed his fiddle to bits." He looked sadly at Officer Bryant.

"I'm sorry to hear about that." Officer Bryant looked bewildered. "But who is Peewee?"

Peewee had never seemed important enough to me to tell Officer Bryant about him. Now Chester told him all about finding the old-time musician to teach us "Whispering" and about his working for Mr. Rose.

"He's the most scared guy you ever saw," Tracy told him. "When that guy next door shows, Peewee ducks out."

"Peewee calls Mr. Rose the bossman," I told him.

"Yeah?" Officer Bryant suddenly began patting the pockets of his jeans and pulled out a notebook. "Anyone got a pen?"

I handed him mine and he began making notes. "What does this Peewee look like?"

"Oh, he's not such a peewee," I started. "About . . ."

"Five feet eight or nine, I'd say," Chester finished.

"What color hair?" asked Officer Bryant.

Peewee's hair was kind of a no-color. We looked at each other.

Chester took over. "Mixed gray and blond—what there is of it. And his eyes are pale blue. He weighs maybe one forty."

"Good!" Officer Bryant told Chester. "Now, let's start on Mr. Rose."

We told him the best we could. How big he was, his high-waisted trousers, cigar, diamond ring, black Cadillac.

Officer Bryant took it all down. " 'The bossman,' you say Peewee calls him. Who does he boss? Have you seen anyone else around there?"

"Are you kidding?" asked Tracy. "Only about a million people."

"Right! But I mean in the daytime."

The guys looked at me. "Peewee trimmed the ivy in front. A guy helped Peewee lay out the parking lot, but I haven't seen anyone except in service trucks driving up there since those first gangster types we told you about."

Officer Bryant looked at the boarded-up windows. "Too bad you can't see over there."

I handed him my knife to pry the plug out of my knothole and he called back to the guys, "Douse the candle, someone."

Now and then we could hear the soft swish of those expensive cars going up Mr. Rose's driveway. It was old stuff to us now, so we just sat around in the dark waiting.

Officer Bryant took quite a while. At last he said, "Okay, you can light up again," and came back to study us. "Got anyplace to play besides the next Poverty Palace contest?"

"Sure," Tracy said. "Frank's mom is having a party for her hospital guild."

"When is that?"

"Next Saturday night," we told him.

"Is that a large group?" he asked.

"It's going to be a big bash," I said. "We'll have torches up the driveway—a lot of people."

"That will mean lots of cars."

"Yeah, But they'll have to park on the side streets. We don't have Mr. Rose's parking lot."

"Next Saturday night. Let's see—that's Saturday the thirteenth. Right?" Suddenly I thought he seemed a little tense. "I'll try to be around to help with the parking." He turned back to the group. "How about running through a few? What was that you were playing when I came in?" He took his guitar out of its case and we all tuned again. I watched each of the guys look toward Bob's place to make sure he was still there.

As he sang with us, Officer Bryant really seemed to relax and enjoy it. We sang the "Wabash Cannon Ball" and some others he'd sung all his life. We kept it up until we all felt warm and happy and hated to leave.

17

Gassed!

Everything had been so fine with Officer Bryant that in spite of Peewee's warning about Mr. Valentine we went back to our room that next night. We had forgotten to practice "Whispering" when Officer Bryant was there and Saturday night was Mom's party.

It was already dark, and the night was broken by the occasional dim glow of headlights passing by the bushes lining Mr. Rose's driveway. The sounds of music, voices, and laughter drifted over from the party as we unlocked our door. Chester lighted a fresh candle, fitting it into the neck of the Coke bottle. Tracy lovingly polished and tuned his bass. The rest of us tuned, leaning against our positions at the table, but being careful to leave Bob's spot at the end waiting for him.

Tracy fingered a long low chord and we began our usual ritual with "Will the Circle Be Unbroken?" as we watched Bob's place. Our wild shadows flung themselves against the wall and I began to get a funny feeling. It seemed to me that Bob was there and then he wasn't. I sneaked a look around at the guys—at Woody singing in his rich low voice, his guitar slung around his neck, at Chester peering through his glasses toward Bob's place, his hair flying out as he fiddled. Tracy plucked the bass and his big baby face looked sort of silly in its seriousness.

Was Bob really there? Were we, all of us, kind of sick hanging on to him like this? Suddenly I couldn't stand any more of it. I switched to "Whispering" and broke the spell. Tracy gave a big, relieved sigh, and just for a second there I thought his breath caused the flame of our candle to waver. We turned, hands lifted from our instruments, toward the door, from where something had been thrown into our room with a thud. Then the door closed. Metal clashed over metal, there was a click, and we knew a padlock had been clamped over the hasp. We were locked in!

Everyone began shouting. Tracy ran to the door, twisting and pulling on the handle. Chester grabbed him around the middle and they both pulled. They crashed to the floor, with the door handle in Tracy's hands.

Woody and I had leaped to the spot where we'd heard the thud. It was a tear-gas cannister and it was fizzing and emitting horrible fumes. We kicked it to the end of the room as Woody screamed, "We're gassed!" and began to choke.

My nose, eyes, and throat burned so much I could hardly bear it, and my mind flashed from the broken windows Peewee had nailed up so securely to keep out birds to the door into Mr. Valentine's house with the board across it and no doorknob. Luckily it was at the other end of the room from the sputtering cannister. Tracy and Chester remembered it too and, coughing and gasping, we all rushed through the smoke to force the board off. We all tried, but pushing wouldn't open the door. When Woody saw me pull out my Swiss army knife, he held the candle for me so I could find the screwdriver blade. It was like working under muddy water with my head on fire until I found it and knelt by the door. Blindly I slipped the screwdriver close against the shaft of the door handle. I'd done this before to open our sun-room door. It worked! The door popped open and I drew in a big breath of clean air from the long black hall that lay ahead.

Woody, his guitar slapping his back and the candle in his hand, rushed into the hall. Tracy with his bass thumped after him. Chester and I, blinded and coughing, felt for our instruments and followed. Although I pulled the door closed behind us, the gas filtered through, but it was a lot better. Even so I couldn't get my breath to yell at Woody. We had passed the closed door to the other wing, and I figured we were near the kitchen where we could break a window and get out. Chester and I had just caught up to the other two so that I could grab Woody's arm and point when this awful feeling hit my middle and I threw up all over everyone. Before they could hassle me about that, there was the sound of a shot, followed by crashing glass in the kitchen.

We froze in panic. Then, on tiptoe, we turned to go on but the hall seemed to end. The spot where we stood throbbed with our pounding hearts. I began to shake and gag. My eyes burned so that I could barely see the candle. We seemed to be trapped. Then Woody and the candle disappeared. Creeping ahead I saw he had found the stairs leading up to the servants' quarters. My eyes burned and my heart raced as I stumbled after the hollow thump of

Tracy's bass. At the top of the stairs, I forced my eyes open and saw Woody trying the handle of a locked door. The sound of wood splintering below petrified us. Heavy footsteps followed!

Then we all saw the hall turned left, opening into the front of the house. We raced down there. Remembering the balcony over the front porch, I pushed ahead of everyone.

A dim light from the street came through the still-intact glass doors that led onto the balcony. The footsteps were coming up the stairs as all of us charged the doors. They sprang open. We were outside at last and the warm glow of lights from my house was right there across the street.

"Dad!" I screamed, my seared lungs making it come out thin and high. "Dad! Help!"

Then all of us were yelling. But we might as well have been halfway around the world. Dad and Mom were at the back of the house watching television.

Woody rushed to push the doors to the balcony closed. He braced his back against them and yelled for Dad. We joined him and even with our yelling we heard men's voices cursing behind us. Then heavy footsteps thumped away.

We were still yelling when Tracy left us and crept along the ledge outside the balcony. Suddenly he leaped back in, picked up his bass, and dropped it over the side. We waited for the sound of smashing wood, then we all climbed onto the ledge. Tracy's bass was still swaying on top of a big bush. I found another bush and dropped my banjo. Woody and Chester did the same. But it was much too far to jump.

I felt the guys watching me as I remembered the big front pillars. Running my hands over the side, I found a pillar's curved surface. With more nerve than I've had before or since, I swung myself over, wrapped my legs and arms around it, and slid all the way to the ground. Man! Nothing ever felt as good as that ground under my feet!

I ran out so the guys could see me and one by one they followed.

Then we were at the top of our steps with the hose turned on. We couldn't get enough water to cool our raw throats and bathe our burning eyes both. Officer Bryant's motorcycle pulled up and he turned his headlight on us.

"Hey! Where were you when we needed you?" Tracy yelled.

"I came as fast as I could when I found out about what's going on over there. Don't you kids ever go near Mr. Valentine's again, you hear?"

"Now you tell us!" Woody shouted.

"What happened?" Officer Bryant asked.

"Well, it wasn't the Smoky Mountain Boys," I said.

"First we got locked in, then gassed, then shot at," Chester said. "If we hadn't started yelling for Frank's dad, I don't know what would have happened."

"Whew!" Officer Bryant whistled. "As bad as that? But you're okay?"

"Just barely," I said. I felt as if I might get sick again.

"Who did it?" Chester asked.

"I'm right sorry about all this," Officer Bryant stamped down on the bike starter. "Stay away from there! Tell you about it later." He roared away.

Woody looked after him. "Some friend!" he said.

"Yeah," we all echoed, "some friend!"

But I was feeling very guilty as "some friend" bounced around in my mind. I was "some friend." I felt really sick at my stomach as I watched the guys take another drink from the hose and head for home. They were such great guys and I hadn't leveled with them about being certain it wasn't the Smoky Mountain Boys. I had been so hung up on not losing Bob's ghost that I'd risked all our lives.

Now I forced myself to think back to the funeral. Each step of the way I went over it, from the time Mom told me Bob was dead to sitting in the church, carrying the coffin, watching it being lowered into the grave.

I cried a little out there in the dark in front of my house and it made my eyes and throat burn, but at the end when I listened for Bob's high mandolin playing in my head all I could hear was a distant car. I felt a whole lot better when I brushed myself off to go into the house.

18

The Party

The guys had decided to give Mom's party the full treatment. We had found old-fashioned vests to wear with our gold-rimmed spectacles and counted on Tracy's act to break the ice. After all, we had a brand-new audience.

All that day things were being hauled up and left in our yard. A dance floor was laid over the badminton court (really our parking space). A carpet of green fake grass was rolled out over the lawn, and white Japanese lanterns were hung over lights in our trees. Then tables with pink cloths, bright flowers, and candles were spaced around under the trees.

Mom and the other guild members kept me busy moving tables, distributing ashtrays, and setting up chairs. Even after the guys had arrived they thought of things for us to do. There were caterers and all, but Mom and the rest of her guild knew just how they wanted things. It was all pretty exciting.

We worried about the dance band that was going to play.

111

They would probably be like most people and think blue-grass was for the birds.

When the people began arriving we stood around and watched for a while. Mom and Dad greeted them. The guests were all dressed up and in the mood for a party, and they kept telling Mom and Dad how great everything looked.

Mrs. Flanigan came in laughing. "Now how did you manage that? There's a policeman out there to show us where to park our cars!"

We remembered that Officer Bryant had said he would be around. All of us looked sideways at each other. Then we decided to grab some stuff from the kitchen and go up to my room to eat. We had our own party.

Woody wandered over to the window and looked out. "See how different things look from here," he said.

We all joined him at the window. Everything looked so strange with the torches lighting up our driveway and the guests pouring in. Cars lined both sides of the street and some even were directed to park in the side streets so that the people could come here.

I felt sorry for Mr. Valentine's neglected Venetian palace, so dark and forlorn. I thought of how much it had meant to us and how lonesome it looked. We were never going there again and just for a second there I had a wild idea that maybe, now that Bob was really gone, the sound of our music would haunt our room.

Finally the crowds began to dwindle and we got bored with watching. Tracy, Chester, and I picked up our instruments and started tuning, but Woody still stood there looking out. "Quick! Come look at this," he suddenly yelled over his shoulder. "There's a police car turning up Mr. Rose's drive."

We rushed back to the window.

"There's another turning up the side street by Mr. Valentine's!"

Then, still another police car drove into Mr. Rose's drive and stopped dead. A Mercedes that had slowed—obviously to turn into Mr. Rose's—sped on down the street.

"Man!" Chester shouted. "Looks like that creep, Mr. Rose, is in trouble!"

"Let's go!" called Tracy, already halfway out the door.

We all rushed down and stood on the curb watching. Nothing more seemed to be happening. Two more cars took off in a hurry when they saw the police car flashing its lights in the driveway, but that was all.

Finally we gave up and went back. Our party was going great. I found Mom and asked her how long it was before we were to play. She told me to ask the orchestra when they wanted a break. I looked at them sitting there in the light and didn't have the nerve. I looked for Dad and he asked them. He came back checking his watch. "About ten minutes, they say. That will be ten thirty. Okay?" He shook my arm the way he does when he is feeling friendly.

"Just right," I said. "That will give us time to tune."

We charged up to my room, swilled down another Coke, put on our vests, and found our glasses. Then we started tuning.

Tracy was nearest the window. Even with our tuning there was a hum of motorcycles outside. "Wow! Come look at this!"

We gathered in the window. Motorcycle police were

slowly riding down the street at intervals of about thirty feet. They turned up the side street and, it seemed, were circling Mr. Rose's block. The police car with its light flashing and radio blaring still stood in the driveway.

"Whew," whistled Chester. "It's got to be the entire police force out there!"

Then Dad was calling us and we went down. He led us among the guests to where the dance band had been, picked up the drummer's stick, and struck the cymbal. The rumble of conversation dropped and Dad announced into the mike: "I wish to present the Indestructible Old-Time String Band. They're going to play some bluegrass music." He turned to us. "What are you going to play?"

We were all moving around getting into position. It didn't seem we were getting enough attention to put on our act with the glasses, so Woody took the mike and said, "Daybreak in Dixie," and we began playing.

The people near us turned to watch and listen, but those farther back only half turned and pretty soon their conversation began to hum again. We didn't know what to do.

During the sprinkling of applause, we decided to give them one more of our favorites before we played "Whispering." Woody announced "Fisher's Hornpipe." One of those life-of-the-party bald-headed men in the back started a little jig to this and the group around him clapped to the beat. A few others turned back to us. This was a little better, so we got up the nerve to try a song: "Black-Eyed Susy." This seemed to be about enough, so during the sparse applause I shook my head at Woody and he announced, "The following number is in honor of our host and hostess: 'Whispering.' "

This brought a little polite attention and I must say they

looked happier with us. We played it first with the fiddle tremolo. Woody took it on Bob's mandolin. We were going to end with my syncopated banjo picking breakdown.

Just about then two police officers—one of them Officer Bryant—appeared at the edge of the crowd. Dad made his way through to them and we could see them go into a huddle. As we finished Dad made violent motions for us to come over.

The dance band was returning now, and the players clapped with the rest of the guests as we filed out. At a signal from Dad, the music started up again. Almost instantly the dancing resumed, so that only a few curious looks were cast at the police officers.

When we got there, Dad told us, "Your friend, Officer Bryant, here, and Captain Jackson say they need your identification of the people who live across the street."

We all stared at him bug-eyed!

19

Captain Jackson

Officer Bryant introduced us all to Captain Jackson, who was no older than my Dad, but kind of gray and patient looking, with a no-nonsense way about him. He quickly led the way out. The noise of our party began to fade.

We whispered to Officer Bryant, "What's going on at Mr. Rose's?"

He just shook his head over his shoulder and stopped by our front door. "Put your instruments away and come along."

We got rid of our instruments and followed the men down our steps.

Talking over his shoulder, Captain Jackson told us, very soberly, what was expected of us. "I don't like to embarrass you boys, but there will be a group of people, and I want you to pick out the persons known to you as Peewee and Mr. Rose. I have it set up so you won't confront them. This is a very serious matter and we are in a position of having to depend almost entirely on your identification.

Officer Bryant, here, says we can rely on you. You are quite certain you know these two men?" By the blinking lights of the police car he turned to face us.

Suddenly we all felt pretty frightened and grim. "Yes, sir, we know both of them."

"One of you was face to face with Mr. Rosseti, so Officer Bryant tells me, but it was at night. You are certain you would know him again?"

"Mr. who?" I asked.

"Rosseti," Captain Jackson said. "This is the Rosseti gang, and his alias is Rose. Would you know Mr. Rose?"

"Oh, yes, sir!" I said. I tried to sound mature. "I couldn't forget him. Besides, all of us saw him from the window when he was pacing off his pool—parking lot. We thought it was going to be a pool."

We were up the driveway far enough so that even in the dark we could point out the windows of our room.

Captain Jackson looked up at them. "It's all boarded up."

"We have a knothole," I said. It sounded kind of silly.

But Captain Jackson just said, "We'll check that out later."

Right about then a Continental started moving slowly down the drive. Ahead of it walked two policemen. They nodded to Captain Jackson in passing. "We got the information," they told him.

Then, as slowly as a funeral procession, other cars drew into line behind the Continental and the faces of all the passengers looked as if they were on their way to a funeral.

Captain Jackson strode past the cars and we followed closely behind Officer Bryant. He turned back to us just as we came into the light on the steps to whisper a clue. "Ever been to Las Vegas?"

So that was it! Our eyes popped open even wider as we looked at one another. Sylvia Maars and all those people who came to Mr. Rose's came to gamble!

We followed on into the beautiful long room I remembered. The sparkling crystal chandeliers were lighted. Suspended from the ceiling over the green felt-covered tables were mirrors in which dice and numbers and squares on some of the tables were reflected. There were smaller tables, too, with cards scattered on them. Partly filled glasses stood here and there. I smelled the blue tobacco smoke still rising from the ashtrays but it was all mixed with the perfume of the ladies who had just gone.

The police officers led us on to where glass doors closed off a room being used as a bar. Captain Jackson motioned us to stay back as he walked past the door, turned out the light, and returned to us.

"Now, just wait a few minutes," he said. He and Officer Bryant stationed themselves in front of the doors and looked into the room. In the dim light we huddled at the side, listening to a lot of men's voices inside the room.

Suddenly the Captain said, "Now! Come up behind us and point to Mr. Rose and Peewee."

We crept up and looked into the room. It was brightly lighted and filled with people—police officers, several men in white jackets, and a great many more in dark suits. Captain Jackson must have waited until the men answering the descriptions we had given Officer Bryant were in view. There stood Mr. Rose holding an unlighted cigar. A police officer, pad in hand and pen poised to write, looked up at him.

Perspiration gleamed on Mr. Rose's forehead. His diamond flashed as he pounded his fist into the palm of the hand that held the cigar. He was roaring, "I have ab-so-lute-ly no in-ten-tion of giving you a statement!" He glared down at the policeman. I felt like running again. He really looked ugly!

Then I saw poor old Peewee. He was next to Mr. Rose, staring up at him with his pale eyes. He looked just the same—kind of scared. The only time he ever had looked any other way was when he was fiddling his heart out.

"That's Mr. Rose," we said. We hated to say it, but what could we do? "That's Peewee—right next to him."

Captain Jackson motioned us away from the door and strode in. Everyone turned to stare at him. "You can take them now," we heard him say.

Officer Bryant herded us outside into the dark shadows by the steps to wait. We saw them all being led out—handcuffed, every one of them. Officer Bryant explained some of it as we stood there. "When you boys told me about a party every night, I reported to Captain Jackson, head of the vice squad. We found the same cars parked on the side streets every night, so we chose this evening for the raid, when Frank's parents were having a party and the streets would be easy to block off."

"Were they getaway cars?" asked Tracy.

"Right," said Officer Bryant. "If you are feeling unhappy about your friend Peewee, this same setup operated in a Beverly Hills mansion a couple of years ago. He's been through it before. They served a little time. The Rosseti gang has smart lawyers."

Just then Captain Jackson came out. "Let's check on the

view from your knothole." He started to lead us through the bushes. "You stay here, Bryant, so I can spot you."

When he got to our door he took out an all-purpose tool, opened it to a screwdriver, handed me the flashlight to hold over his work, and removed one side of the hasp. He opened the door and I led the way with his flashlight and showed him the knothole.

He peeked through it for a moment. "Okay," he said. "I see him clearly."

We all went back again to rejoin Officer Bryant.

"That about does it," said Captain Jackson. "Thank you, boys, for your help. We may have to call on you later, but I doubt it." He started back toward Mr. Rose's. "Officer Bryant will see you home."

We crowded around Officer Bryant, full of questions. But two men, one with a camera, appeared from behind Mr. Rose's house. "Hold it, will you?" Just as we turned around, a flashbulb dazzled us. The other man came up to get our names. We didn't know what to do.

Officer Bryant answered for us. "This is the Indestructible Old-Time String Band. They have been practicing nearby and were able to identify the ringleader of this gambling outfit."

The reporters started to close in on us, but Officer Bryant held up his hand. "We've had a big evening and I'm sorry, but you will have to excuse us. Come on, boys." He shoved us gently ahead of him and followed us down the drive explaining. "Valentine's been mixed up with Rosseti for a long time. He lost a bundle in the Beverly Hills operation, and when he couldn't pay off they vandalized his house. Rosseti had him over a barrel when he moved next door. Of course Valentine had plans of his own—he was trying every way to get Mrs. Merrifield out so as to combine his property with hers for a real estate deal. That's where you came in, along with the cow and packing boxes. The noise you made helped break up her home for the aged."

"Then they weren't her aunts?" I'd always wondered how she could have so many aunts.

"No. This neighborhood is strictly residential zoning—no nursing homes allowed. When she moved, I think Mr. Valentine would have locked you out—remember the padlocks? He was too cagey to let me in on his plans, so—"

"Then Mr. Valentine set the fire, threw the cherry bombs, and chased us through the house?"

"No." Officer Bryant sounded worried. "And that scares the hell out of me. It was the Rosseti gang. First they set the fire and Valentine raised a fuss with Mr. Rosseti. How was he going to pay them off if they burned his house? Of course Valentine wasn't leveling with Rosseti—he had a fortune in paintings and furniture—some of it stored in the house. By reporting the fire you saved them for him, so he was glad to have you there, but he must have known you were in danger."

We still couldn't figure it out. "The cherry bombs and—?"

Officer Bryant went on. "After the fire, Peewee was put in charge of getting you out. You were lucky—he didn't want you hurt. He—"

We began to laugh. "Peewee! He did all that crazy stuff?"

"Reckon so."

"But that wasn't Peewee—the tear gas and the shot. We heard their voices," Chester said.

"No," Officer Bryant explained. "I figure Rosseti caught on to the police prowling around at Valentine's." He turned to Woody. "That's probably what made the ceiling fall. Rosseti sent over some real mobsters to get rid of the snoopers."

Now it all made sense, and poor old Peewee had tried to protect us.

What is left of the Indestructible Old-Time String Band still gets together. But now Tracy is gone. His family moved to Georgia and we won't see him until next summer, when he comes to visit his grandmother. We are all into different things—Chester's taken up serious music and Woody's playing the lead in the school play. I've been helping Curtis with his Chevy and I'm in with a whole new group of guys playing basketball. Maybe that's on account of my growing so tall.

When the band gets together we sometimes play "Whispering" and then think of Peewee. And we always play "Will the Circle Be Unbroken?" and think of Bob. If Officer Bryant isn't there to play Bob's part, Chester, Woody, and I take turns on the mandolin because we can't hear Bob playing with us any more. We still get some of that warm front-porch-back-porch feeling when we're together, but it's not quite the same now.

Everything is changing. They are going to tear down Mr. Valentine's house. But sometimes at night, when I look out my window at his lonesome old Venetian palace, I remember the wonderful bluegrass music we used to play. Then I've just got to sit there picking my banjo for a while because I'm never going to forget the Indestructible Old-Time String Band.